LOVE at SECOND SIGHT

Also by Cathy Hopkins

Million Dollar Mates series

Million Dollar Mates
Paparazzi Princess
Catwalk Queen
Golden Girl

And, coming soon . . .

Super Star

Other series by Cathy Hopkins

Mates, Dates
Truth, Dare, Kiss or Promise
Cinnamon Girl
Zodiac Girls

Cathy Hopkins

LOVE at SECOND SIGHT

First published in Great Britain in 2012 by Simon and Schuster UK Ltd
A CBS COMPANY

1 3 5 7 9 10 8 6 4 2

Simon & Schuster UK Ltd
1st Floor
222 Gray's Inn Road
London WC1X 8HB

Simon & Schuster Australia, Sydney

Simon & Schuster India, New Delhi

A CIP catalogue record for this book is available from the British Library.

PB ISBN: 978-0-85707-550-5
eBook ISBN: 978-0-85707-551-2

Typeset by Hewer Text UK Ltd, Edinburgh
Printed and bound in Great Britain by
CPI Group (UK) Ltd, Croydon, CR0 4YY

www.simonandschuster.co.uk
www.simonandschuster.com.au
www.cathyhopkins.com

In the beginning, one soul split into two creating soul mates. And ever the two shall wander seeking each other.

Unknown

Chapter One

It all started on May bank holiday weekend.

It was Friday afternoon and I trooped out of school with my best mates, Effy and Tash. Despite the grey skies and threatening rain, they were in a sunny mood, unlike me.

'Three whole days off to hang out with Dave,' said Tash.

'Three whole days to hang out with Mark,' said Effy.

Three whole days for me to be Miss Tag Along, I thought as they talked over plans on the way to the bus stop. It was the first bank holiday of the month and once again, I'd be the odd one out. *All by myself*, as Bridget Jones sings in the movie.

'Oh, and to hang out with you too, Jo,' Effy added. 'We wouldn't leave you out.'

I tried to look enthusiastic. I knew I'd be included in any plans. They're good friends and we all know the rules when dating boys: mates come first. Even so, it isn't a ton of fun going to the movies, all five of us, with me wedged in between two couples, not knowing where to look when they snog each other's faces off. Then going for pizza and watching them feed pepperoni to each other across the table while I sip my Diet Coke and try not to look like a sad loser. Or evenings spent at each other's houses listening to music, while Mark and Effy or Dave and Tash send slow smiles between them across the room as if to say, 'Don't we have something special here?' while I, feeling left out, wonder what I'm doing to put boys off and whether there's something wrong with me because my relationships don't last.

So, no. Another weekend of being reminded that I'm single is not my ideal, that's for sure. Not that I haven't had boyfriends. I have. I even made a list of them in my diary one night when I was home alone to remind myself that I'm not a total reject.

My *love life so far*
by Jo Harris

Jamie

He was back in Year Eleven. I liked him a lot until a small problem came up. He was also dating Cheryl Wilson from Year Ten.

Doug

Also in Year Eleven. He was good company but as time went on, I realised that I paid for everything. Basically he was a cheapskate. I don't get that much pocket money and I thought it would be nice if he bought the cinema tickets once in a while, because it wasn't as if he didn't have any money, he just chose to spend it on CDs or computer games.

Lawrence

He was at the beginning of the Lower Sixth. He could be interesting and funny but was a bit of a dopehead. We didn't last long because I got bored of watching his eyes glaze over and listening to the rubbish he spouted when he was stoned.

Finn O'Brady

I should really cross him off. He belongs more on a wish list than as part of my love life so far. I know he's a total waste of time because loads of people fancy him and I doubt he even knows that I exist. He's the lead singer in a band called Minted. They're a group from the Sixth Form at St John's School for Boys who have become really popular after a promoter turned up at one of their gigs last summer. Now their music is being played on the radio and I even saw them in a teen magazine last month. Finn is cute as hell, with girls lining up for him. I met him when Effy and I signed up to be part of a team putting together a magazine called *Chillaxin*. There are six schools involved, all from around the north London region. Finn's the editor. Not that I knew that at the time. I almost passed out when Effy and I turned up for the first meeting and saw him there. So far, I don't think he's even registered me.

And that was the list apart from Owen so, all in all, my love life so far has left me with a feeling that boys just do your head in.

Owen is the exception. He's Effy's older brother and is away at Nottingham university at the moment. We were a couple for a while, for a few months last summer in fact, but he always felt more like my brother than my boyfriend. He's a nice guy, very grown up for a nineteen year old and protective. 'You're perfect for each other,' everyone said when we were dating. 'So many shared interests. *So* alike.' And they were right. We could talk for hours about books and music, the world and how we were going to change it. We *did* have a lot in common, but someone who's the same as me isn't really what I want. Kissing him was like eating plain yoghurt. Good for you but bland. And he used to have a shiny spot on the end of his nose which, though I know it was shallow of me, I couldn't help but focus on whenever he puckered up and moved in. I just thought, ew, pass me the Clearasil. Not exactly how I imagined true love's kiss to be.

OK, so maybe a relationship isn't going to be like a Disney movie, with a heart formation of bluebirds tweeting away in the background, but surely it wasn't too much to ask for someone colourful and exciting? And scorching hot. I wanted someone who'd burst into my life like a flame and challenge me. Make me think. Turn my insides to liquid honey and make my toes curl. Though that sounds like a case of E. coli. What I mean is, I want to *feel* something. A pull. A longing. Desire. I want Heathcliff from *Wuthering Heights*, wild and passionate. Or maybe not . . . He was a nutter with mad hair and obsessed with Cathy's ghost. Someone like him would be way too high maintenance as a boyfriend. Who else sounds right. . . ? Edward from *Twilight* – the most dangerous and charismatic boy in the school? OK, maybe not him, either. Someone who drinks blood for kicks is probably not the most suitable guy and, anyway, vampires are so last decade. I can't kid myself. I know exactly who I want and his name is Finn O'Brady.

No. *No.* I will not waste time on someone who has a line of girls after him. What would I be? Number sixteen? Seventeen? One hundred? Oh, I don't know. No, I *do* know. I want to meet my soulmate. I want to meet a boy who makes me feel alive like I've never felt before and who feels the same way about me – but I'm not convinced that's going to happen where I live in north London. Most of the local boys (apart from Finn) wear those falling-down jeans that show their bum cracks and Calvin Kleins. *So* not sexy, at least not in my book.

'I think I might stay in and catch up with some study,' I said as the girls discussed going to a movie.

'No way,' said Effy. 'Why don't you want to come with us?'

I shrugged.

'Because you're a singleton?'

'Ish. Look, I'm cool with it. You guys go. Have a good time.'

'You don't need to be single, Jo. You could have boyfriends,' said Tash. '*Loads* of boys fancy you.' She pulled her red beret out of her rucksack, put it on and tucked her hair up into it. Her real name's Anastasia, but we call her Tash. She has shoulder-length, Titian-red hair that goes frizzy in the damp weather. 'Bane of my life,' she always says. She carries her beret everywhere in case of showers, which is a shame because I think her hair suits her curly. No-one's ever happy, though. Effy has long, silky blonde hair and she curses about it being so fine. My hair's dark, dead straight and halfway down my back, and I'd love to have Tash's waves, whereas she's jealous of me and Effy being able to just 'wash and go' without battling with the GHDs.

'Yeah. You're way too picky when it comes to boys,' agreed Effy.

'I just don't want to compromise, that's all.'

'I don't think you should, either,' said Tash. 'I think you should wait for The One.'

'Oh, get real. I mean, we all want to meet The One,' said Effy, 'but until you do, you should get some experience. Practise your snogging!'

And so it went on as we waited for the bus. Same old Friday conversation. Same ole, same ole. It's not that Effy and Tash aren't romantic. They are. Way more so than me, in fact. Out of the three of us, I'm the one with my feet most firmly on the ground. I'm planning on studying journalism (the main reason I signed up for *Chillaxin*), which means thinking rationally, researching ideas, getting facts. Tash and Effy on the other hand are more keen on art and literature, so are encouraged to live in the realm of imagination and dreams. I'm right brain, they're left. Effy is an Aries and, even though I'm not as into astrology as she is, I can see that she's typical of the sign and rushes into things at full speed with great enthusiasm. Tash is a Pisces, the sensitive dreamer, and I'm Taurus. Stubborn, says Effy. I prefer to focus on the other qualities, like loyal, practical and sensual.

Whatever the explanation, we're different, but our friendship seems to work despite that. Effy is also a giggler. It's one of her most endearing qualities. It's so easy to make her laugh. Ever since I met her back in junior school, Effy has cracked up at the most inopportune moments, in assembly for example, when Mrs Burton, our headmistress, says something about stealing in the cloakroom or we have a guest speaker talking about their passion for a cause and we're all supposed to be focused and taking it seriously. Effy's shoulders will start shaking with silent laugher. She tries to hold it in but usually fails. And that tends to set me and Tash off too so we all end up in detention for being giddy. Effy's also endlessly curious. As well as astrology, she's into clairvoyants, tarot cards, visualisations and anything alternative. Miss New Age Nutjob, I call her. My mum's into all that stuff too. She and Effy get on like a house on fire. Most times, I just switch off from both of them when they start ranting on about life and all its mysteries.

Effy glanced at a poster on the wall by the bus stop. 'Hey, look. The fair's coming to the Heath this weekend. Tell you what, let's go on Sunday afternoon. The boys are playing footie that day, then meeting up with mates afterwards, so it would just be us. We could go to the fair, have some girlie time, win a few teddy bears then head back to yours, Jo, for a sleepover. You in?'

I knew Mum was working late on Sunday night so it was either the fair and a sleepover or staying home alone. 'Sounds like a plan. I'm in.'

Chapter Two

By Sunday, the rain had gone and it was a glorious sunny afternoon as we made our way over the Heath for the fair. The good weather had brought out the crowds and the atmosphere was buzzing. Effy spotted the clairvoyant's tent almost immediately. She was like a bee to honey. She linked arms with me and pulled me over to read the small sign tacked outside: *Betty – Past-life readings, Tarot cards and Palmistry. Ten pounds a session.*

'Ten quid to have your fortune told. Come on,' said Effy. 'Maybe she'll tell you if there are any boys in your future.'

I rolled my eyes. 'I bet she tells everyone there's a tall, dark stranger on the horizon. Honestly, Ef, you don't really believe in all that rubbish, do you?' I don't know why I asked. Of course she did. She was always consulting the cards, the runes, the I Ching or the stars. Last month, she did my horoscope for me online. She wasn't happy when I said that if I met a boy it would be because I'd made an effort to get out there, not because Venus was in conjunction with the moon or whatever.

'Oh, don't be a cynic,' said Effy. 'It's only a bit of fun. Pleeease.'

'Yeah, come on, Jo. Let's give her a try,' said Tash. 'Our neighbour, Mrs Adeline, said there was a clair-voyant here last year who was brill.'

'Waste of time,' I said. 'I can think of way better things to spend my money on.'

'Then it's on me,' said Effy. 'An early birthday present.'

My birthday is the 2nd of June, which was less than a month away. I'd much rather get some bath products or a CD but I didn't want to appear ungrateful or hurt her feelings so I eventually gave in.

Effy went first and came out fifteen minutes later. 'She's good,' she said. 'You're next and I've paid for you.'

I looked at Tash. 'No, you go next,' I said. 'I insist.'

'Chicken,' said Tash, but she went in all the same.

'So. What did she say to you?' I asked Effy as we waited.

She shook her head. 'I'll tell you when Tash comes out. We'll compare notes. I don't want to put anything into your head.'

'So it was rubbish, then?'

'No. No. Um . . . nothing that specific, though. I'll tell you later.'

She went and bought us two candyfloss sticks and refused to be budged any further. Ten minutes later, Tash came out with a big smile on her face.

'Don't say anything,' said Effy. 'Not till Jo's been in. Off you go.'

I took a deep breath and entered the tent. It was dark inside and smelt of sandalwood from a joss stick that was burning in the corner. A middle-aged lady was sitting at a small fold-up table which had a crystal ball and a deck of cards on it. She didn't *look* like a clairvoyant. She looked ordinary, with short grey hair, a ruddy complexion and a boring outfit of blue shirt, floral skirt and sandals.

She glanced up at me. 'Jo?'

I nodded.

'Sit,' she instructed and indicated I should take the seat opposite her.

'Give me your watch,' she commanded, so I took it off and gave it to her. She held it in her hand and closed her eyes. After a few moments, she opened her eyes. 'I feel sadness – and also resistance. I feel scepticism, but this will change.' She handed me a deck of cards. 'Think about what you'd like to ask, then shuffle the cards.'

'I . . . there's nothing I want to know specifically.'

'Just shuffle, then,' said Betty. 'The cards will reveal all.'

I did as I was told.

'Now split the cards and put them into three piles from the right.'

Again I followed her instructions.

Betty took the top cards from the middle pile and laid them out in front of her. She studied them for a while, then glanced at me. 'Give me your hands,' she said. I put my hands out and she took them in hers, turned them palm up and studied them. She closed her eyes for a few moments. The atmosphere was intense and I felt slightly spooked. Betty let go of my hands and put hers over the crystal ball. Again she closed her eyes. *I wonder what baloney she's going to come out with*, I thought as I glanced around the interior of the tent.

I caught my reflection in a mirror at the back. A tall, slim girl with brown eyes stared back at me. I was wearing my jeans with my favourite jacket: plum velvet with a nipped-in waist and tiny buttons right up to the high neck. I got it for Christmas last year from my favourite shop, Steam Punk, and have worn it constantly ever since. I love the clothes there, they're kind of Victorian Gothic. I've asked for a pair of the ankle boots from there for my birthday from Mum. The Catherine Victorian boots. Black with a delicate heel, unlike the clompy ones that are in the shops at the moment. Effy says I look like Bellatrix Lestrange from the *Harry Potter* movies. The cheek. Effy and I just have different tastes in clothes that's all. I like old-fashioned, while her style is more Topshop's latest.

Betty's voice brought me back from my fashion fantasy. 'Jo,' she said.

'Yes.'

'You haven't found love in this lifetime, have you?'

Effy's been filling her in, I thought as I shook my head. *I'll kill her when I get out of here.*

'No. Not exactly.' I laughed. 'But hey, I'm only sixteen!'

Betty didn't laugh, in fact she had a strange look on her face. Her eyes had glazed and, oh Lord, she was starting to sway slightly. *Should I make a run for it?* I wondered as I checked behind me for the exit. 'You have travelled far through time to be here. There is no coincidence, it is all predestined.' Betty closed her eyes, became still and started to speak in a deeper voice. A voice that had authority. 'You have not found love, but you will.' *Me and a thousand others*, I thought although I couldn't help but listen and stare. Betty was putting on a good act. 'You can find love, Jo. The reason you have not so far is because you have it imprinted in your unconscious that love is painful and that is why you have not found your soulmate. In this lifetime, you must break the pattern.'

Whoa, I thought. *That's way heavy. She's right about me thinking love is painful but imprinted in my unconscious?* I did *not* like what I was hearing. I glanced back at the exit flap. Half of me wanted to run, but the other half was intrigued. I decided to stay. At the very least I could have a good laugh about it later with Effy and Tash.

'I see a boy – you once knew him and he was your soulmate,' Betty continued. She spoke fast, still in the deeper voice. 'It was a great love. Powerful. He was your true love in a previous life. We have all had many lives but this love was in your last life. You were a governess . . . your name was Henrietta Gleeson. You were working in a London doctor's house at the end of the nineteenth century. This doctor had children. Two. A young boy who you were employed to care for, and an older one . . .' She lifted her head slightly to the right as if she was listening to someone. 'Howard. His name was Howard. A boy of nineteen. He was your soulmate and yet . . .' She stopped, as though listening once again. 'Something happened to keep you apart.'

Typical, I thought. *Bad luck in this lifetime and bad luck back then too. Cool story, though. I wonder how many other people she's spun it to.*

Betty opened her eyes and looked directly at me. As if she was looking right *into* me. 'Jo. This is important. As you are back in this lifetime, so is he. Like you, he has travelled far through time to be here. In this life, you must find him. He is your soulmate. You are meant to be together. You *must* find him if you are ever to be happy in love.'

I felt a shiver go up my spine, but I wasn't going to let her get to me. 'Was he by any chance tall, dark and handsome?'

Betty continued to look directly at me. 'You may scoff at what you hear, many do. I simply tell what I see. It is always *your* choice to make of it what you will but this boy from your past, he *is* your destiny. You can believe me and try to find him or dismiss what I say and drift from one meaningless love affair to another, never finding the true contentment that your soul could know with him. You must choose.'

Whoa. You're beginning to freak me out, I thought, then we both jumped as someone entered the tent to our right. It was a blonde lady in her twenties. 'Are you still doing readings?' she asked Betty.

'Have you any more questions, Jo?' Betty asked me, returning to her normal voice.

I shook my head. I felt light-headed. 'Um. No, thanks. I'm fine.' I got up and Betty beckoned the lady to take my place. *Another sucker,* I thought. *I bet she even tells her the same story.*

Chapter Three

'Oh my God, that is just *so* romantic,' said Tash after I'd filled her and Effy in on the Howard and Henrietta story.

'Did she say what kept them apart?' asked Effy.

I shook my head. 'Maybe he discovered he was gay.'

Effy ignored my comment. 'But didn't you ask her how you'd recognise him this time?' she asked as we made our way over to the stage area. Minted were due to play at three o'clock and I wasn't going to miss that. A chance to stare at Finn O'Brady without seeming weird.

'No I didn't, Effy, because Betty *made* it up.'

'He could be anywhere,' Tash mused. 'He might not even be in England. What if he's American or something?'

'Effy. Tash. There is no *he*. There's no-one to find. You don't actually believe it? She probably tells every-one the same story. Who did she say you'd been in your past life? Cleopatra?'

Effy shook her head. 'She didn't mention past lives at all. She told me I needed to focus on what I want to do when I leave school. That I have a tendency to start and stop things, not see things through.'

'Well, she got that right,' I said. 'But no mention of soulmates or anything?'

'Nope. Nadah. I wish she had.'

'Nor me,' said Tash. 'She told me that I would probably go abroad in the future and that it would be a good experience.'

'Gap year. That one's easy,' I said. 'She guessed your age. Loads of people travel before college or uni so it's not hard to put two and two together there. Hey, did she do the deep voice and swaying?'

'No,' Effy and Tash chorused.

'What deep voice?' asked Tash.

'Like she was possessed. Bit spooky if I'm honest but I guess it's part of the act. Did she *really* not do it when you were in?'

Tash and Effy shook their heads.

'It was probably her spirit guide coming through. Loads of mediums have them,' said Effy. 'Usually Native Americans or great souls.'

'What if it was the spirit of Ethel, the dinner lady, or Fred, the dustbin man?' I said. 'Why do the guides always have to be exotic?'

Effy shrugged. 'I don't know. They just are.'

'I think what she said sounds wonderful,' said Tash dreamily. 'Someone you've known in a past life. Maybe even lots of past lives. A love destined to be time after time.'

'Oh, come on. I mean look at me, Tash. Look at my jacket, my style. Victorian, vintage. She took one look at me and that set her off. Because I dress like this, she made up a story about me being a governess in Victorian times. She must take her clues from people's appearance. She's got a good imagination, I'll give her that.'

'But maybe that *is* why you dress like that, Jo,' said Effy. 'Because you were Henrietta and you're still stuck in the past.'

I couldn't believe what I was hearing. 'God, you two are so gullible, you'd believe any old tosh. I simply like vintage style. Me and hundreds of others. Does that mean we were all Victorians in our last lives?'

Effy looked put out. 'Maybe.'

I rolled my eyes. 'I despair. The here and now, that's all we've got, Effy, the present moment and Minted are about to play. I'm going to forget all about what Betty said and go and get a good place to listen and enjoy the rest of the afternoon. End of.'

Effy glanced mischievously at Tash. 'OK. Lead the way . . . Henrietta.'

I playfully went to swipe her but she ducked. 'Nutjob,' I said.

Chapter Four

Finn O'Brady. Tall, fit, tousled black hair, a teenage girl's dream. He had charm, charisma, a wicked twinkle in his dark brown eyes, and knew how to work a crowd, directing some of the slower numbers to girls in the audience. He even sang some lines to me. As he looked into my eyes, I felt the words right down to my toes. Maybe he had noticed me at the magazine meetings after all.

'Maybe he's Howard,' whispered Effy.

'Hope not. He's way too full of himself to be good boyfriend material,' I said as Finn turned away from me and directed the rest of the song to a stunning girl with long dark auburn hair in the middle of the crowd. She had a tender look in her eyes as she smiled back at him.

'I think she's with him,' said Tash. 'I saw them together before the band went on stage.'

The girl looked every inch a rock singer's girlfriend in a tiny denim skirt and cowboy boots. *I should have known he wouldn't be single. Not that I care*, I thought.

'Hey, look,' said Effy. 'The bass player. Isn't that Ben?'

I looked over to where Effy was pointing. 'Ben who?'

'Ben Fraser,' replied Effy.

'He was the year above us in junior school. Bit of a loner.'

'Can't say I remember him, junior school was a while ago,' I said as I looked over at the boy Effy was talking about. He was tall and slim with dark, longish hair and was wearing shades so I couldn't see his face properly. I must have seen him in some of the magazine shots of the band though, and never really taken much notice. Finn was the only one I registered.

'He's on the *Chillaxin* team as well, you must recognise him from there?' said Effy. 'He was at one of the meetings. I think he takes photos for the magazine. I *knew* he looked familiar.'

'If he looks familiar, maybe he's *your* soulmate,' I teased as I turned my attention back to Finn.

'Familiar because he went to the same junior school as us,' said Effy. 'Not familiar as in my love destiny.'

'Methinks the lady doth protest too much,' I said.

'I'm not protesting,' she objected.

'You-oo love him. I'm going to tell Mark.'

Effy thumped my arm. She's so easy to wind up sometimes.

The band struck their last chords, took a bow and made their exit. I noticed the girl with auburn hair make her way backstage and couldn't help but feel a stab of jealousy.

Tash pointed at a row of stalls to the side of the dodgem cars. 'Let's go and look over there,' she said. 'I need to get something for my parents' wedding anniversary.'

We followed her over to the stalls selling lavender soaps and bath gels.

'Finn's family are looking for a house in Highgate,' Effy said to me, as she picked up a soap and inhaled the scent. 'Mum told me.' Effy's mum runs an estate agency up in Highgate village so she always knows all the gossip about who's selling and who's buying locally. 'She said they're looking for a three-bedroomed house with a garden room or studio. Probably for Finn, don't you think? For his band.'

'He'd have pretty fab parents if they were actually looking for a home studio for him. How do you know his dad doesn't work from home, or his mum?' I asked. 'The studio could be for one of them.'

'I don't,' said Effy. 'I was just speculating.'

'Hmm. You speculate about a lot of things without having all the facts, don't you, Effy?' I said.

'I so do not. Like what?'

'Like now with Finn's parents and before, running away with what the clairvoyant said to me.'

'Ah. So that's what's bugging you,' said Effy.

'It's not bugging me. I'm merely pointing out that you get carried away by your own imagination sometimes.'

Tash stood in the middle of Effy and me. 'OK, you two, pack it in,' she said, always the peacemaker.

I wasn't sure why but I felt grumpy and I could see by Effy's frustrated expression that I'd got to her too. Maybe the clairvoyant had unsettled me, not with the Henrietta story, more because she'd been accurate about me feeling that love was painful. That was true, especially after having just seen Finn with another girl.

'It would be cool to know where Finn lived though,' Tash said, 'then you could accidentally-on-purpose bump into him, Jo.'

I turned my nose up. 'He has a girlfriend. Anyway, not interested.'

'Yeah sure,' said Tash.

'You could camp in his garden,' suggested Effy with a grin.

'Yeah and get carried off by the police for stalking along with all his other groupies,' I replied. I looked back at the stall. 'Anything here, Tash?'

She shook her head. 'Mum might like bath stuff but I doubt if Dad would appreciate it. Any other ideas?'

'I'll have a think,' I said as I watched Finn and the auburn-haired girl walk past us. He glanced over and looked me up and down, like he was clocking my jacket, and gave me the briefest of nods. Despite my promise to myself that I wasn't going to get into him, I felt my stomach lurch pleasantly when his eyes met mine. *Damn*, I thought as I turned away.

A moment later, Effy nudged me. 'Finn's coming over.'

I turned back and indeed, Finn looked like he was heading my way. I felt like my brain was about to fuse. I wanted to talk to him but also didn't, not if he was with another girl.

'Hello, Jo,' said a voice to my left.

I turned to see Mrs Rayner, an older lady who worked as a volunteer at the same hospital as my mum but had recently retired. 'Oh. Hello, Mrs Rayner,' I said as I glanced over her shoulder. Finn had noticed that I was talking to someone and turned around, walking back to the girl he was with. I felt torn. I so wanted Finn to come over but I liked Mrs Rayner and wanted to talk to her too. She was a sweetheart who would chat to me and make me a hot chocolate if ever I was waiting at the hospital for Mum after her shift. I hadn't seen her for a while so we spent a few minutes catching up and by the time we'd said goodbye and she went off to join her friend, Finn had long gone.

Effy squeezed my arm. 'Forget Finn, we'll find you someone else,' she said and began to scan the crowd at the fair then nudged me to look over to the rest of the band. By now, they had packed up their equipment from the stage and were walking out towards the exit. Ryan, the lead guitarist, Josh, the drummer, and Ben Fraser, the boy Effy had pointed out. I noticed that Ben had a black Labrador on a lead. He stopped to adjust the dog's lead. I had a feeling he had overheard Effy say Finn's name but it was hard to tell because he still had his shades on.

'Yes. There will be others,' Tash added.

'I don't want anyone else,' I said.

Even behind the shades, I felt Ben look at me, his face registered disapproval. Maybe he thought I was just another saddo fan on a very long list. He tugged on the dog's lead and walked away.

'I mean, I don't want *anyone*,' I said loudly so Ben could hear. Even though I didn't know him, I didn't want him thinking I was a loser. 'I'm happy being on my own.'

Effy and Tash both burst out laughing. 'Yeah, looks like it.'

Effy wasn't going to give up. 'So. Let's think. What's your type?'

'I don't know. I don't know if I have a type.'

'Yes you do,' said Tash. 'Haunted, Victorian poet with dishevelled hair; in fact, just like Finn.'

'In that case, that is *so* not my type,' I said.

Tash laughed. 'Oo, Little Miss Petulant.'

I stuck my tongue out at her.

'Whatever, we have to find Howard,' said Effy.

'Oh, shut up about Howard and Finn. I mean, just for a moment, say Betty's story is true, then he could be anywhere on the planet – in India, Australia, Outer Mongolia – not right in front of us on the Heath, five minutes after I've seen a clairvoyant!'

'Ah so you *do* think there might be something in it?' asked Effy.

'*No*. Course not. But if it was true – and it *isn't* – it's just not very likely that he'd be the next boy I see, OK?'

'But if he's your soulmate,' insisted Tash, 'you'll surely find each other. It's meant to be.'

'Says who?'

'Your *destiny*,' said Effy.

I scoffed. 'Yeah right. But if you put that garbage about Henrietta and destiny aside, I do like to think that I have a soulmate somewhere but *not* someone from another life. I want someone in *this* life.'

'So go and talk to a few boys,' said Tash. 'Be positive. You're the one who's always saying you have to make things happen.'

'OK, I will,' I said. I glanced around but there wasn't one boy in sight who vaguely took my interest. 'Er, but maybe not today.'

Luckily Effy and Tash didn't push it any further. We continued browsing the stalls.

'Do you think Mark is your soulmate?' I asked Effy.

She shook her head. 'I like him a lot, but I think he's Mr Right Now instead of Mr Right Forever.'

'I think Dave is my soulmate,' said Tash. 'It was like

we recognised each other when we met. In fact, the first thing he said to me was, "Where do I know you from?" But we hadn't met before that first time. Maybe I knew him in a past life and that was why there was something familiar about him.'

'Yeah,' I said. 'Maybe he was your pet goldfish.'

Tash laughed, but her and Dave did have something special. They had been going out since Year Eleven when Dave arrived at our school. Effy and Mark on the other hand were a much more recent couple; they'd only been dating a few months.

'So what do you think is a real soulmate then?' I asked them. 'Someone you fancy like mad? Someone you're drawn towards but you don't know why? How *do* you recognise The One when you meet him?'

'I think it's how he makes you feel. Like, it's right but exciting at the same time,' said Tash. 'Like a vibe.'

'Chemistry,' I said.

'And you can't stop thinking about him,' said Effy.

'And when you're apart you can't wait to be with him,' added Tash.

Exactly how I wanted to feel with a boy. I just didn't want him to be a boy from beyond the grave. That was just too spooky.

*　　　*　　　*

After the fair, we went back to my place for a DVD and a sleepover. My house is nothing special. It's a mock-Tudor semi-detached on a quiet street between Highgate and Muswell Hill. Three bedrooms and bathroom upstairs and two rooms that have been knocked through to make one big living room and a kitchen downstairs. Faded white walls, Ikea furniture and rugs and a few posters around the place. One is a seascape with dolphins, another is the Field of Poppies by Monet. Every year, Mum and I make a resolution to buy some new artwork but somehow it gets forgotten as the routines of Mum's job and my school term take over. That night, Mum was on the night shift at the hospital where she works on the admittance desk in A & E so we had the place to ourselves.

After pizza and a fourth viewing of *Bridesmaids*, we went up to my room where I have made some effort with the decorating in an attempt to make it my space, although it's three years or so since I did it. The walls are a dark red colour and I've got Pre-Raphaelite posters on the wall. I love that era of art. Ophelia floating on her back in the river by Rossetti. King Cophetua and the Beggar Maid by Edward Burne-Jones. Echo and Narcissus, Hylas and the Nymphs, both by John Waterhouse.

Effy looked at the pictures. 'See, even your posters are from the past, Jo. All tragic ladies.'

'Not all of them.'

'They look pretty tragic to me,' said Tash as she scrutinised the posters.

'I like them because they're romantic,' I argued, 'and the colours are so vivid. Plus you have to admit, all the boys in them are lush, just look at them – high cheekbones, great hair, not like the spotty oiks that hang around here.'

Effy pointed at the painting of Hylas and the Nymphs. 'This one looks at bit like Ben, the bass player from Finn's band. Good cheekbones.'

'Hah! I knew you loved him,' I said.

Effy picked up a pillow from my bed and threw it at me.

'And this one looks like Finn,' said Tash, pointing at the Burne-Jones poster. It was true, the king in the painting did have a look of Finn. Dark with black eyes that twinkled like polished gemstones.

I shrugged. 'OK. So maybe I *do* have a type, except it's not that Ben bloke. He looked well miserable. I swear he scowled at me earlier on the Heath.'

'You'd make a good pair then,' said Effy. She pulled a sad face.

'I am so not miserable,' I said.

'Only teasing,' said Effy. She looked back at my posters. 'I wonder what Howard looked like.'

I rolled my eyes and sighed. 'I thought we'd forgotten about him.'

Effy shook her head. 'No way. In fact, I've been thinking about what Betty said to you and if you're not going to do anything about it, I am. I'm going to look for Henrietta.'

I laughed. 'Look for her? But *I'm* supposed to be Henrietta so you don't have to look far.'

'No, dozo. I mean the actual Henrietta. If she did exist, then there will be records of her, like when she was born, where she lived, those kinds of things.'

'Don't waste your time. Betty probably told a dozen single women at the Heath this afternoon that they were Henrietta Gleeson. I bet she did exist and was Betty's great-aunt or something.'

Tash nodded. 'Possible.'

But Effy had her 'I won't be budged on this' face on.

Tash threw herself back on my bed. 'So it might be a story that Betty tells everyone, but you still have to admit it's romantic,' she said. 'There's no harm in just looking for Henrietta. See where it takes us.'

'It would have saved a lot of time if a boy had been in to see Betty today too and she'd told him that he was Howard and then she could have said, "Ah, I've just seen Henrietta. *What* a coincidence. Quick, get out in the fair and find her."'

'You've just got a closed mind,' said Effy. 'A cynic.'

'Whatever,' I said and began to make up their beds on the floor.

Later that night, Tash woke me. 'Jo, Jo, it's OK. I'm here.'

'Wha . . . Who?'

'You were calling for your dad again.'

I looked at the clock. Three a.m. I wasn't surprised. Effy and Tash had been woken by me during many a sleepover over the years because of a recurring dream that I have. I can never remember the exact details of what happens in the dream, just a sense of loss and an old house, a house that I don't recognise. Effy, Tash and Mum have all told me that I call out for my dad. He died of a heart attack when I was nine years old. It was totally out of the blue and I still really miss him. Mum's made me go and see so many sleep specialists over the years to try and stop the dream. She's had me try lavender oil, counting sheep, relaxation techniques starting with my toes and up through my body. None of them have helped much because it's not that I have a problem *getting* to sleep, it's that I wake up when I have the dream and then can't get back to sleep. Mum's latest fad is for me to try hypnotherapy. She sits in the waiting room reading magazines whilst the therapist puts me under and I have a nice kip – feels like that anyway. I've had three sessions so far and it seemed to be helping a bit, that is until tonight.

'Want me to get you a drink?' asked Tash.

'No. I'm fine. Sorry I woke you. Go back to sleep.'

Tash settled back down.

'Maybe we've heard wrong all these years,' said Effy from the depths of her sleeping bag on the floor. 'Maybe all this time, Jo hasn't been calling "Dad", she's been calling for Howard – Howa-dad. Get it? Howa-d . . . ad. Sounds similar.'

I pulled a pillow out from behind me and threw it at her. 'You really do have an overactive imagination,' I said as it landed neatly on her head. 'I call out for my dad. Always have. So forget about Howard-ad. That's just wishful thinking on your part.'

'Whatever,' said Effy. She turned over so that she had her back to me.

I snuggled down again. Somehow I had a strong feeling Tash and Effy weren't going to let the Henrietta story go, no matter what I said or thought.

Chapter Five

'Oh, tell the whole world, why don't you?' I said as I squeezed into a seat beside Tash and Effy the next morning at our favourite café on Highgate High Street. We liked it up in the village; it had an old-world charm, with Georgian terraced houses built around the square where just about every teenager in north London liked to hang out. There were a few individual, quirky shops there as well as a good number of cafés where we could meet up to check out who was around and who was with who.

Mark, Dave and Owen were wedged in opposite and I'd heard them discussing my visit to the clairvoyant when I walked into the café, even though they had all fallen silent when I sat down. I had thought about telling Mum about it before I left the house earlier but before I could get a word in, she'd laid into me about leaving pizza boxes all over the place and not clearing up after Effy and Tash had gone. She was never in a good mood after working the late shift at the hospital so it clearly wasn't the time or place to have had a girlie talk about soulmates or clairvoyants.

'Hey, Owen,' I said. 'What you doing back from uni?'

'Quick visit, I only got home last night. Needed my laundry doing. I'll be going back tomorrow,' he said, then gave me a suggestive look. 'So. About what the clairvoyant said. I might be your Howard.'

'And why's that?' I asked.

'I'm in my first year of medicine. Howard was the son of a doctor.'

He looked miffed when I laughed out loud.

'Seriously though,' said Mark. 'I saw a programme about reincarnation on telly once and there were some very convincing cases.'

'On telly, hey?' I replied. 'Must be true then.'

This time it was Mark's turn to look put out. 'There was a woman on the programme who'd been doing research into past life phenomena,' he went on, 'and she had some fascinating case histories. Especially kids. Apparently many recall their past lives but the memory fades after the age of five. Some of them remembered places, people and events they couldn't possibly have known, and when they checked out the details, it was just as the kids had said.'

'I saw that programme,' said Effy. 'There was an Indian boy who insisted that he had a shop and family in a different village to the one where he was born. In the end, his parents took him to the village and there was the shop and family just as he described and he was able to tell exactly what changes had been made to the shop since he died. He knew all about the place and the wife who ran the shop came to accept the nine-year-old boy as the incarnation of her departed husband.'

'Amazing,' said Tash.

'Mad. The boy probably read about it in a newspaper or something,' I said. 'And that's why the facts check out. Kids absorb everything around them.'

'Take no notice of her,' Effy said to Tash. 'She's such a cynic. There were loads of examples on the programme of people remembering things from past lives that they couldn't possibly have known. One young girl said that in her previous life she had buried some jewellery, and when she took her new family to find it, it was buried exactly where she had said.'

I rolled my eyes. 'I'm sure that there's a rational explanation for all the cases you saw but then that doesn't make good telly, does it?'

'I despair,' said Effy. 'But anyway, we've come up with the most brilliant idea.'

'Yes. I've thought of a great present for my mum and dad,' said Tash.

Phew, I thought. *Change of subject from past lives, thank God.* 'What's that?' I asked.

Tash gave Dave a coy look. 'It was Dave's idea. I'm going to do a family tree for both of them. You know, find their ancestors.'

'That's a lovely idea, Tash. They'll love that,' I said.

'Family tree. Ancestors,' said Effy; she gave me a meaningful look and added, 'Census records, Jo. They're on the Net.

'Yeah. I know. You can get them online now.'

'I don't know why we didn't think of it earlier,' said Tash.

Effy nodded. 'Don't you get it, Jo? Henrietta. We can look her up while we're researching Tash's roots.'

Ah, I thought. *So we haven't changed the subject. No such luck.*

'They have records of births, deaths and marriages,' said Dave. 'We can find out everything about her and even maybe the doctor she worked for. He would be listed on one of the census records. They were recorded every ten years from 1841 and you can see all the records up until 1911, so everyone living at a certain address on the night of the census was recorded. If we're going to find anything out it's a great place to start.'

'But it's this life that matters, surely? Not a past one. Even if I did believe in past lives, it's gone, over,' I protested. 'And anyway, we don't know where they lived.'

'London,' said Effy. 'You told us Betty said London.'

'Think of it as a project,' said Owen. 'Research. It could be interesting.'

'I can think of better things to research,' I said. It wasn't like Owen to be into something like this. He usually took the scientific approach to life. Maybe he and I didn't have so much in common after all.

The door to the café opened to our right and Tash nudged me. 'Don't look now but. . .' Course Effy and I immediately swung round to see who'd walked in.

Finn O'Brady.

41

I turned away quickly. So uncool to be seen ogling, no matter how much I wanted to. Not Effy though. She carried on staring. I saw Finn notice her and he turned his back as if he didn't want to be seen. He bought a drink then slid into the only place available, which was a table across from us.

'I'm going to speak to him,' Effy said and got up.

I tugged on her arm. 'No. Leave him. He probably just wants to blend in. It must be so tiresome being recognised wherever he goes.'

Effy pulled away and went over to Finn's table. 'Hi,' she said. 'I just wanted to say that I,' she pointed to the rest of us who were all trying to assume indifference but were listening in at the same time, 'I mean we, we all think your band is brilliant.'

I couldn't resist looking to see his reaction. He flashed Effy a killer-watt smile. 'Thanks,' he said then looked down and stirred his drink. Anyone with an ounce of sensitivity would have taken his body language to mean, Thanks, now move on. Effy, however, has the sensitivity of a dead dog.

'Do you get fed up of people recognising you?' she persisted.

Finn looked up again, shrugged and smiled, weakly this time. 'Part of the job.' I thought he looked trapped because he glanced around as if seeking an exit. He was so good-looking, it was hard not to stare. *Stands out from the crowd*, I thought as I tried to drag my eyes away but didn't succeed. Totally my type, as Effy would say.

Luckily Effy, Tash and I all have different taste in boys. Dave is tall and pale – he looks like he lives underground which is probably because when he's not with Tash, he rarely comes out into the light and spends his time in his basement on his computer playing sci-fi games. Tash thinks he's deep and mysterious. I think the words 'a bit gormless' are more apt, but each to their own. Tash hangs on his every word. She probably has to because he doesn't say that many. Mark's medium height and cute in a Harry Potter way with glasses and dark hair that has a will of its own. He can't quite believe his luck in having someone as pretty as Effy as a girlfriend, which is probably a good thing because she bosses him around something rotten. Because he's so in awe of her, he obeys without question. Owen's sweet-looking, though he'd hate to hear himself described that way. Like Effy, he has an open, friendly face with a wide mouth that's often smiling. Finn however is in a league of his own. *Probably full of himself, most mega handsome boys are*, I thought as his eyes scanned the café. He saw me looking at him. I didn't want him to think I was another on his long list of his admirers (even though I was), so I got up, seized Effy by the neck of her shirt and tugged her away.

'Excuse my friend,' I said to Finn. 'We don't let her out often because she doesn't know how to behave in public. Do you, Effy? Come on now, sit back down. It's time for your medication.'

By now, most of the café was staring and Finn laughed. 'Hey, it's cool . . . Don't I know you from somewhere?'

I blushed. 'Er . . . yes. I'm part of the *Chillaxin* team. I've been to a few of the meetings.'

Finn nodded. 'Oh yeah. Course. In fact, we should have another meeting soon. We need some new, original ideas for articles for the next edition.'

'And I saw you play on the Heath yesterday.'

'Oh yeah,' he said and pointed at my jacket. It was the one I was wearing yesterday. 'I like the way you dress. So you saw the set?' I could see he was waiting for me to say something about his band.

'Yeah. Um . . . quite good.'

Finn laughed again. 'Quite?'

'Yes. I thought some of the songs were a bit similar.' A warning voice in my head told me to shut up.

I always do this when I speak to a boy I fancy – try to sound cool but end up sounding like I'm being critical. *So* not the same thing.

Effy knows me well and could see I was in danger of saying something stupid. 'You've also seen *me* in my mum's estate agency,' she blurted out.

Finn looked at her and nodded. 'Oh right,' he said.

'Yeah. Two doors down. Davis Reed?'

'Oh right! My parents are looking for a new place, preferably with an outhouse or soundproof garage so I can rehearse.' He smiled and Effy flashed me a 'told you so' look. 'I don't think they can stand my music any more. They don't even think it's *quite* good.'

'It's not that bad,' I said, then put my hand over my mouth. 'I think I might shut up now.'

'Good idea,' said Effy. She turned to Finn. 'See, it's Jo who needs the medication and doesn't know how to behave in public. Not me.'

'I also think I'll go and sit down now,' I said and for some inane reason, I bowed. *Bowed?* Albeit a small one. More of a bob. When I got back to our table, Tash was looking at me open-mouthed.

'So . . . yes . . . that went well,' I said. 'Where are the boys?'

She indicated outside the café window where Owen, Dave and Mark were now hanging out. 'Don't think they liked having competition.'

The café door opened again and two tall, leggy girls entered, spotted Finn and went over to him. One of them was the girl he was with on the Heath, the other had long blonde hair and looked so posh she could have stepped out of the party pages of *Tatler*. Probably an Arabella or Cordelia. She looked down her nose and gave Effy a look as if to say, *Who the hell are you?*

This time Effy did get it. 'OK, later,' she said to Finn.

He grinned. 'Yeah, later.' I could see that he liked being seen with an admirer by the two girls. *God, he's so transparent*, I thought.

Effy scuttled back to join us. 'I think he likes you,' she whispered. 'He remembered you from yesterday.'

'He remembers my jacket,' I said. 'And now he certainly won't forget me from today. He must think I'm an idiot! Anyway, it looks like he has a girlfriend, maybe even two.'

Effy was never one to give up. 'Might not be serious,' she said.

I shook my head. 'I'm so not interested. I think he's arrogant. Probably got an ego the size of a bus.'

Opposite me, Tash was making 'zip it' signals and shaking her head.

'What?' I asked.

She pointed behind me. I turned to see that while I'd been talking, Finn had got up from his table to head for the counter. He must have heard every word I said.

'Jo was talking about someone she saw on telly, not you,' Effy called to him, making it a thousand times worse.

'Sure,' he said. Like he believed her. Not.

We finished our drinks and headed out of the café to join the boys. Our plan for the day was to mooch around the shops, which is one of my favourite things to do, but we quickly found that everything was closed because it was a bank holiday. Instead we had to make do with a bit of window shopping. At least the boys seemed happy about having escaped being dragged into every single shop.

A book in the window of an antique/junk shop caught Owen's eye as we passed by. 'Give me a mo,' he said as he peered in the window. The others went ahead but I waited for him and together we looked at the usual mix of stuff on display: odd bits of china, paintings, frames and trinkets.

Owen pointed to a sepia photo in a silver frame showing a young woman from the Victorian era standing next to a pillar with a plant. 'Hey look—'

'Don't even say it, Owen,' I interrupted.

'Say what?'

'That she might have been Henrietta. Ever since yesterday, that's all I've heard from Effy and Tash.'

'Ah well, you know my sister. She has a vivid imagination,' he said as he peered at the photo. 'And I wasn't going to say that. I was about to say it's a nice frame, but come to think about it, yeah, imagine just for a moment that the story the clairvoyant told you is true. Imagine looking at a photo of yourself in a previous life. OK not the one in the window there, that would be way too much of a mad coincidence – but say you found a photo of the real Henrietta—'

'That's if she even existed.'

'Yeah but imagine it – that the spirit looking through the eyes out of the photo is the same spirit that's looking down through your eyes at it. Just different bodies in different times.'

'Owen! That's so creepy. Effy's not the only one with a vivid imagination in your family.'

Owen laughed. 'Just speculating.' He paused to looked at me. 'I was only teasing before, you know, when I said I might have been Howard. Listen, Jo, you know that Effy's like a dog with a bone when she gets into something. We've all seen it before. Let her do her thing and chew away until she gets bored. This will play itself out and she'll move on to the next thing soon enough, but in the meantime, look at it as a bit of fun, otherwise you guys are going to end up arguing.'

'I guess. We have both been winding each other up over it. She gets so mad that I won't just accept the idea and I get mad with her for not questioning things more.'

'The saying "What you resist, persists" was never truer than in Effy's case.'

I nodded. 'Yeah.' I knew my friend only too well. When she got into something, she tried to take us all with her, and if I was honest, her enthusiasm for life was one of the things I loved about her. Life was never dull around Effy, like the time she insisted I had a ritual to symbolise the end of my relationships with boys who were a waste of time. She told me to get a photo of all of them and we burnt them. She put the photos in a pan which she placed on the coffee table at their house but the flames got out of hand and we almost set fire to the curtains. She likes a ritual, does

Effy. She'd have made a good witch. Owen was probably right. The more I resisted, the more she'd press me. To go along with it was the best way to let her get it out of her system. 'So do you believe in reincarnation?'

Owen shrugged. 'I don't believe and I don't not believe, if you know what I mean. I really don't know. I guess the only way to know for certain is to die and find out, that's if consciousness carries on in any way. I like the idea of rebirth though, you know, that the soul or spirit never dies and that we just cast off our bodies at the end of one life, like a set of clothing at the end of the day, then, just like we wear new clothes the next day, we pick up new bodies and carry on.'

'Very deep, Owen.'

He laughed. 'That's me. Deep.'

I laughed too. Ahead of us Dave was strolling with his arm around Tash; Effy wasn't far behind with her arm linked through Mark's. As Owen and I sped up to catch them, I thought again about how well Owen and I got on. I felt like I could talk to him about anything and he just *got* me.

A black Golf went past. I turned to look and saw Finn in the back seat; the two girls from the café were in the car too. *Maybe I should reconsider Owen as boyfriend material*, I thought. *A boy like Finn would do my head in. He has so many girls after him, I'd always be watching my back and wondering if I could trust him. I can't imagine having a proper conversation with him about something serious like I've just had with Owen, though maybe that's not fair seeing as I've barely spoken to him at all. Anyway, it's ridiculous to even think about it, Finn's way out of my league.* I made myself focus back on Owen. Just thinking about Finn filled me with a sharp pain. Owen, on the other hand, was comfortable, easy to talk to and always had something interesting to say.

I thought about his idea of changing bodies being like changing clothes, that the body is a wrapping but not the real us. It made me remember how I'd felt when Dad died. Mum had taken me to see his body. I didn't want to but she thought it would be good for me – a closure of sorts. It certainly took away any fantasies that he might walk back in the door. I turned to Owen. 'When I saw my dad after he'd died, I remember saying to Mum, "Dad's not here." I don't think she knew what I meant, but it was so clear to me that his body was like an empty shell. What made Dad *Dad* had gone. He'd gone and left his body behind, so yeah, I get what you were saying about the body not being the real person.'

Owen took my hand as we walked on together in silence, both lost in our own thoughts. Even silence was easy with Owen.

Chapter Six

I arrived in the school library the next day to see Tash and Effy already hunched over the computer. We'd agreed to meet there during the lunch break to start researching Tash's family tree.

Tash's face was flushed with excitement as I walked up to them. 'Jo,' she said. 'We've found something.'

'Great,' I said. 'On your mum or dad's side?'

'Not her parents. We're looking for Henrietta,' said Effy.

'No way! You haven't found her?' They couldn't have. She didn't exist unless I'd been right and she was a relative of Betty's.

'Not exactly Henrietta, but we've made a start. We've found a family of Gleesons.'

'But what about the family tree for your parents?' I asked Tash.

'This is way more exciting,' said Tash. 'Don't you think?'

I had to admit part of me was intrigued even if only to discover that Henrietta was Betty's great-aunt or her great-aunt's cleaner. There had to be a rational explanation. Besides, a family of Gleesons wasn't exactly the same as finding Henrietta.

I sat down beside them. 'OK, show me what you've found.'

'You have to pay for some of the sites, but we found one where we could make a start,' said Effy. 'It asked for a date of birth, which we obviously don't have, so we typed in her name and London and just tried a few different dates. Can you remember anything else that Betty said?'

I rolled my eyes up as if I was going into a trance and spoke in a low, deep voice. 'Speak to me, Henrietta, speak to me from deep in my soul.'

Tash punched my arm. 'This is serious!'

'Shh,' said Mrs Cole, the librarian, from behind her desk.

I remembered Owen's good advice from the day before. What you resist with Effy, persists. 'Sorry,' I whispered. 'No, really, sorry. Show me what you've got.'

Effy passed me a sheet of paper. 'See, so far, we've found a Lucy Gleeson and a John, a Violet, Alice, Cecilia, Thomas, a whole family of Gleesons but they're in Manchester and Ireland, not London.'

I was about to say that didn't prove anything, Gleeson is probably a common name, but I bit my tongue. The new me was going to play along if only for a peaceful life.

'She could have been born there and moved,' I said. 'Chances are she relocated because work as a governess was probably scarce where she lived.'

'Now you're thinking,' said Effy. 'We just need to find a Henrietta. Do you think she changed her name?'

I shook my head. 'No. Why would she do that? Doubt it. Keep looking.'

'Dave said he'd go online at his school if he gets any time too,' said Tash. 'And apparently his uncle is researching their family tree so has access to some of the ancestry sites you have to pay for. Dave's asked him to help too.'

There was no getting out of it. The two of them would enlist the help of the whole world if given half the chance.

'I think we should try some more dates,' suggested Tash. 'I think that's our best plan seeing as we don't have an actual date of birth.'

'OK,' I said. 'Let's think rationally.' *Haha*, I thought. *Rationally. Here's me researching a woman that I supposedly was in a past life. How rational is that? Not.* 'What do we know? We know that Henrietta was a governess, we can assume that she wasn't that old because if Howard was the son of the doctor, he was probably a young man, he wasn't going to fall for an old lady—'

'Unless he had a mother complex,' said Effy.

I tried to keep a straight face. They were taking it so seriously. 'Maybe, but let's not go that route for now. Let's assume she was in her early twenties. Betty said it was at the turn of the century, around nineteen hundred. So if Henrietta was in her twenties then she was probably born between . . . 1875 and 1880?'

'Brilliant,' said Effy and went back to the screen.

I went to another computer and used the time to look up my father and soon found him. A date of birth, a dash and a date of death. It made me so sad to think that's all there was of him and nothing to tell of the full life he'd had in between the two dates. A whole life summed up with a dash.

'Found anything?' Effy called. I shook my head

then googled images of Finn O'Brady. I needed cheering up after having found my dad online. When Effy glanced over at me, I quickly found an ancestry site. I thought I'd better co-operate in the search for the Gleesons if only to keep her off my case. I found a few in Liverpool. Annie. Emilia. Jim. Then went back to googling Finn O'Brady. That was much more fun.

Half an hour later, Effy and Tash still hadn't found a Henrietta. I didn't think they would.

As we left the library and got out into the corridor, we turned our mobiles on. A text came through for me from Owen. **How goes the search?**

I texted back. **So far, a dead end.**

He texted back. **Haha.**

Tash had a text too. She looked up from her phone. 'That was Dave to say that he hasn't had any luck in his search either.'

No surprise there, I thought. I tried my best not to say, told you so.

'We need to find Betty again,' said Effy. 'We need more facts.'

'But the fair was only on the Heath for the weekend,' I said. 'She'll have gone.'

'Yeah, but she mentioned to me that she has a stall at Camden Lock some weekends.'

'Did she?' I tried to look enthusiastic. Clearly Effy wasn't going to give up that easily.

Effy nodded. 'We can go and look for her this Saturday and see if she can give us a few more details. In the meantime, maybe Dave's uncle will find something. Apparently he's a whiz at researching stuff on the Net.'

Don't hold your breath, I thought, but I didn't object to the idea of a day out in Camden. It was always buzzing down there and there would be plenty of other stalls besides those of fortune-tellers with vivid imaginations.

Chapter Seven

'Not seen her this way for a long time,' said a man on a vintage clothes stall. 'Ronnie in the café reckons she's gone back up north for the summer.'

It was Saturday morning and, as I'd expected, Betty was nowhere to be found in Camden Lock, though Effy and I looked everywhere and asked a good number of stallholders.

Great, I thought as I feigned disappointment. *Maybe this thing is going to burn out faster than I reckoned.*

We cruised some of the jewellery and clothes stalls at the Lock for a while, had an organic apple juice at a juice bar, then Effy went off to join Tash who'd gone to watch the boys playing football.

'You coming?' she asked.

'I'm good here for a while, thanks. I might look around a bit longer then head home and work on school stuff,' I replied. It was a warm day, good for browsing the open-air stalls, plus I wanted a bit of space away from coupledom and from the Henrietta stuff which seemed to be dominating every conversation.

'OK,' she said. 'Anyway, Tash and I need to discuss your birthday plans.'

It was a tradition with the three of us that we arranged something for each other's birthdays – either a girlie sleepover, a few people over at one of our houses or an evening out for just three of us. We all put a lot into it when it was our turn to be the organisers and it was fun being surprised by whatever had been arranged. Last year, they made me a treasure trail of presents, all hidden in Effy's back garden. The first ones were small, silly presents like my fave magazine, chewing gum, a heart chocolate, a miniature teddy bear, all leading to my main present which was a gorgeous collection of Bobbi Brown make-up. For Effy's birthday, Tash and I arranged a day of beauty treatments. We started the day for her with a bubble bath with scented candles, then we did her nails before finishing with a visit from a proper beautician who gave her a facial. For Tash's, we got tickets to see her favourite band, the Laddites, at Kentish Town. I couldn't wait to see what they came up with for me this year.

After Effy had gone, I cruised a few of the vintage stalls and bought a fab handbag, made from what appeared to be crocodile skin, for eight pounds. I didn't want to go home yet so mooched around a few more lanes looking at the stalls. Everywhere I went, I noticed couples, hand in hand or just sitting chatting, laughing, having a good time. If not in couples, the other people my age were in groups. Friends hanging out, helping each other choose a top or a necklace or a nick-nack, just like Effy, Tash and I used to do before they went into their couple bubbles. I missed our girls only weekends.

As I walked on, I became more aware that there were very few people my age on their own and I felt a pang of loneliness. *Get over it*, I told myself. I would certainly never begrudge Effy and Tash time with their boyfriends and usually I was quite happy with my own company – in fact, I like my space, it was just that lately I seemed to be having rather a lot of it. I looked at my watch. *I could go home and catch up on homework*, I thought, *but it will be so quiet there*. I decided to go and walk down by the canal instead. As I made my way through the jostling crowd, I glimpsed Ben the bass player from Finn's band. He was coming towards me and appeared to be on his own. I waved but it was hard to tell whether he saw me or not because he was wearing shades. Either way, he didn't respond. When he got closer, I made a point of acknowledging him. *It wouldn't hurt to be matey with a friend of Finn's,* I told myself.

'Hey, Ben,' I said.

He stopped but didn't say anything.

'*Hi,*' I said.

He still didn't say anything.

'Quiet, mysterious type, are you?' I asked and gave him a cheeky grin to show I was being friendly not critical.

'Not really,' he replied.

'Ah, so you do speak?'

'Course.'

'I saw you play on the Heath the other Sunday,' I said. 'With Finn O'Brady.'

'Oh yeah. Finn.'

'So you on your own?' I asked. I thought if he was, I might suggest we get a cappuccino. We could join the crowds of chatting teens plus it would be a great opportunity to find out more about Finn, maybe even his relationship status and how serious things were with the girl with auburn hair I'd seen him with on the Heath and in the café.

'No, I'm here with Finn. He's around here somewhere.'

I tried to keep cool. 'Somewhere around here as in at the Lock? Or north London? Or just on the planet?'

He didn't laugh at my attempt to be funny.

This isn't going well, I thought. *Time to move on and maybe I'll bump into Finn myself.* 'OK, well, nice talking to you.'

'Right,' said Ben, and with a brief nod he pushed on past me.

I immediately thought of a nickname for him – Scowler. I made my way down the left of the Lock and through a narrow passage lined with stalls selling posters, badges, lighters and joss sticks. There were loads of boys around looking at CDs and clothes. *Any one of them could be Howard,* I thought, *and maybe we're destined to keep missing each other: I turn right as he turns left or I walk past just as he turns to look in a window. How sad would that be? Whoa! Jo, watch yourself. You're beginning to think like Effy. I'm supposed to be the one that doesn't believe.*

I must have laughed aloud at my thoughts because a voice to my left said, 'First sign of madness that.'

I turned to find myself looking into Finn O'Brady's dark eyes. 'Oh! How did you get here?'

Finn looked amused by my question. 'Probably same way as you. Tube. Feet. So why were you laughing?'

I blushed. I hate that I can't stop it and it gives me away every time. 'I was just thinking of something funny.'

'And what was that then?' he asked as he fell in step beside me. 'You going towards the canal?'

I nodded.

'Mind if I walk with you?'

'No.' I felt chuffed to be seen with him and could see a few girls turn their heads to look at him as we walked past.

'Been shopping?' he asked me.

'A bit.' I held up my new bag. 'Just this.'

'Nice. So just cruising round on your own then?'

'Yes. No. Seen loads of people I know,' I blustered. I didn't want him to think I was a billy-no-mates loser with no-one to hang out with on a Saturday. 'I saw your mate Ben and before that I was with my friend. We were, er . . . looking for someone.'

'Someone? And who might that be?'

'Just . . . someone.'

'Ah. A mystery someone?'

'Not exactly . . . well, sort of. Long story.'

'And is that what was funny?'

I felt awkward. 'Sort of.' I was aware that I was giving him short answers and not being very interesting.

'So share the joke. I could do with a laugh.'

No way was I going to tell him the Henrietta story. He might think I was a nutter or claim to be Howard just to tease me, but he was looking at me expectantly. I had to say something. 'I, er . . . that is . . . a friend of mine, um. . .' I wished my brain would get into gear. *Why is it so easy to chat away with Owen but so hard with Finn?* I asked myself. 'Um, where to start? OK, it all began on the Heath last week—'

Finn put his hand on his heart. 'When you saw me? Everything changed?' He grinned. 'See, you were right – I am big-headed.'

So he *had* heard what I'd said about him having a big ego in the café. 'Before that. I . . . that is, a friend went to see the clairvoyant. . .'

Finn's eyes twinkled. 'A *friend*.'

'Yes. A friend. Effy – you met her in the café the other day? She dragged me along to see the clairvoyant too. Early birthday present.'

'When's your birthday?'

'June 2nd.'

'Doing anything special?'

'I'm not sure yet. Effy and my other friend Tash are arranging something.'

'Sweet. So you were saying. Clairvoyant?'

'We went to see the one on the Heath. The day you were playing. It's Effy who's into all that stuff though, not me.'

'No, course not, not you,' he said solemnly, but there was something about the way he said it that made me feel like he didn't believe me at all. 'Did she tell you that you were going to meet a tall, dark stranger?' Finn raised an eyebrow suggestively.

He's flirting with me, I thought as I felt myself blush again. Like it or not, I did fancy him and there was definitely some chemistry between us, I could feel it down to my toes. It felt like we were walking along in our own rosy-coloured bubble. *Not getting into it, not getting into it*, I told myself. *He has a girlfriend, I've seen him with her so it's out of order that he's flirting with me. I wonder if she knows what he's like? Poor girl. I knew. I just knew it. Boys like Finn just play with girls' heads because they can. Well, he's not adding me to his hit list.*

'No. She didn't.'

'Ah, shame,' said Finn.

'She said that I'd met someone already.'

'Already? So she *did* mention me?'

I felt that Finn was teasing me but I wasn't going to flirt back. 'No, she definitely did *not* mention you. She, er. . .' I didn't want to tell him the whole story but maybe part of it if only to stop him asking questions. 'She said something about soulmates knowing each other through different lives.'

'Different lives?'

He looked genuinely surprised and it felt good to have said something at last that really got his interest. 'As in a past life.'

'You're joshing with me.'

'No.' It was fun to see him look so gobsmacked.

'What else did she say?'

'Um . . . I can't remember all of it. Something about finding my soulmate.'

'Soulmate, huh? Not sure I believe in them.'

'Well, you wouldn't, would you?' I blurted then clapped my hand over my mouth.

'What do you mean, I wouldn't? I'm capable of being romantic, I am, but a soulmate . . . that's heavy stuff,' he said, then put his hand over his heart and gave me a meaningful look, his eyes twinkling. 'So you're looking for your soulmate, are you?'

'No, course not. I . . . I don't know if I believe in them either. Maybe they only exist in books and movies. Anyway, enough about me. Why's your band called Minted? What's that about? Sounds like toothpaste.' I don't know why I felt so defensive all of a sudden. Probably because he appeared to be laughing at me, like I was a dumb pet that made him smile.

'Yeah. It's a neat name, isn't it? Ben came up with it. The rest of the band thought it sounded cool. So tell me more about what the clairvoyant said.'

'She said I would bump into a very annoying boy down in Camden one weekend,' I lied.

Finn laughed. 'Ah, now that would be me, would it? Maybe I *am* your soulmate!'

I grinned back. 'Get in line, pal. I have a few contenders so far.'

'Is that right?'

I wasn't going to tell him there was only one. Owen. And that wasn't serious.

'Oh yes, a long list. But it's Effy who's into clairvoyants and stuff, not me.'

'So you keep saying. But I like the notion that there might be a soulmate for everyone out there,' said Finn. 'Someone to meet when you're ready to do the serious stuff, someone you've known time after time. I think I should write a song about it. It's the sort of thing girls love.'

'How could you write about it if you don't believe it?'

Finn tapped his head. 'I have to think commercially. Think about what people want to hear.'

'Huh,' I said. *I bet*, I thought. *I bet that's what you do with all girls, not just the ones in your audiences. You tell them what they want to hear. Well not me, pal. I'm not falling for it.* 'I think you should write what you believe. Write from your heart if you want to touch people. It's fake to write what you think people want to hear. If you're a real artist you should write the truth.'

Finn looked taken aback by my outburst. *Now I should shut up*, I thought, *shut up, shut up! He'll think I'm a nutjob. Why oh why can't I just be myself? I either talk too little or blather away like an eejit.*

'Maybe. Maybe I just haven't met the right girl yet so have no experience of a soulmate. Maybe I'll write about that.' He gave me another of his amused looks.

69

It made me feel very unsettled. 'Maybe the right girl would change my mind. So were you looking for this clairvoyant that you don't believe in to see what else she had to say?'

I shook my head. 'No. I was trying to have a peaceful life. You don't know Effy. Once she's latched on to something, there's no letting go.'

'*Effy*. OK, if you say so. Well, I think the soulmate idea is lovely. Very romantic. Heathcliff and Cathy sort of thing.' Now it was my turn to look surprised. 'See I do know what you're on about. *Wuthering Heights*. Passion. Yearning. Standing on the moors in the wind and rain in the middle of the night. HeathCLIFF. CaTHEEEE. Dying of pneumonia and haunting each other. All that good stuff.'

Now he's being patronising, I thought. 'But the clairvoyant clearly made it up because she's another one who knows what people like to hear.'

'If you say so,' he said with another of his grins.

'I think I might have to punch you in a minute,' I said.

Finn was almost laughing now. 'Girls often say that to me. Why do you think that is?'

'Because you're infuriating. I hate it when people tell me what I'm thinking; you don't know me or what I believe.'

Finn looked deeply into my eyes in a way that made me blush again. 'So maybe I *could* get to know you.'

'I . . . but. . .' I stuttered as an image of him with the girl from the Heath flashed through my mind – though he did just say that he hadn't met the right girl yet. God, it was confusing. Maybe he was just saying that because he knew it was the kind of thing girls want to hear, like, I haven't met The One but you might be her. 'I'm going to go now before I push you in the canal.'

'Have you thought about seeing anyone about this violent streak of yours? Like anger management classes?'

'I am not violent!'

'Er, you want to punch me and push me in the canal.'

Once again, that mocking expression on his face. What was it about him that made me so mad?

'OK. Going now,' I said and this time I did turn and walk away. I couldn't believe the cheek of him. He knew I'd seen him with his girlfriend, twice even! But he must have met lots of girls who didn't care that he was in a relationship. *Well I'm not going to be one of his groupies, like a Little Miss Available*, I thought as I headed back up to the main road. *He's full of himself, a flirt and patronising. I am so not interested, Finn O'Brady.*

'Good luck with your search,' Finn called after me. 'Let me know if any of them mention me.'

I turned back to him. 'I'm *not* searching. Happy as I am.'

'If you say so.'

I walked a bit further, then couldn't resist turning round again. He turned at exactly the same time.

'I knew you wanted me,' he called.

'In your dreams,' I called back, but we were both smiling.

Chapter Eight

The following week, there was no getting away from Henrietta. On Monday evening, I got home to find that Owen had sent me a badge in the post. It said *Reincarnation is making a comeback.* Very funny. Somehow the story about my clairvoyant experience had even got around school. On Wednesday, before assembly, I heard that Mac Johnson in the Upper Sixth, who fancies himself as a Casanova, had apparently been telling every girl he met that he'd known her in a past life. His latest chat-up line and some gullible girls were even stupid enough to believe him.

I was so glad I hadn't told Finn the full story and prayed that he didn't hear it from someone else. He'd have teased me even more than he'd done when he only knew the vague details. However, he'd obviously been thinking about what we'd talked about because on Wednesday evening, I saw that he'd sent me an email.

Hi Jo

Wondering if what you told me at the Lock might be a great idea for an article for the magazine? Clairvoyants, psychics, fortune-tellers. Girls are so into all that stuff aren't they? Hoping to hear that they're going to meet The One, etc. I'm going to source some local psychics and the like and thought you and Effy could do the research and write it up. I think it could be good. Ben could take some pics to go with what you write, so you could have a chat with him too.

Finn

PS: I'll send you the list.
PPS: Let me know what they say about me.

What a cheek, I thought as I printed it out to show the girls at school. *Let him know what they say about him.*

Such a flirt. But I couldn't deny the fact that I was well chuffed to have heard from him.

I was about to show the email to the girls at break on Thursday morning when Tash's phone beeped telling her that she had a text. It was from Dave.

We've found her. Henrietta Gleeson, born Liverpool 1882.

'No way!' I said.

'Wow,' said Effy.

'Still doesn't mean anything,' I said.

'Course it does,' said Effy. 'It means she *existed*.'

'Yes but doesn't mean that *I* was her.'

'It's a lead,' said Tash. 'At least we can use it to find out more about her. I'm going to call Dave.'

'Now, what were you going to show us?' asked Effy as Tash called Dave on her mobile.

I gave her the printed sheet with Finn's email.

'Hmm. Tell him what they say about him? Brilliant,' said Effy after she'd read it. 'I think he likes you.'

'No way. He flirts because he fancies himself as a playboy. I am so not interested.'

'Yeah right. *So* not interested.'

'I'm interested in doing the article though,' I said.

75

'It will be great for my CV when I apply for journalism courses.'

'It might be fun too,' said Effy. 'We could take opposing sides – I'll be for it, you can be against.'

'No problem there then,' I agreed.

'And I see Ben's to take photos,' said Effy.

'Yeah, maybe he could take some of the invisible guides and dead spirits.'

'Haha,' said Effy. 'And for your information, there are some photos where a spirit has been captured.'

'Yes, they're called set-ups, spoofs, fakes, Effy.'

Effy stuck her tongue out at me. 'Us humans don't know everything, you know.'

Tash finished her call. Her face was flushed with excitement. 'Dave and his uncle are still on the case. He says that now we have a date of birth, they should be able to find a date and place of death too. That should tell us if Henrietta moved from Liverpool and once we know that, they can maybe work out where she lived for most of her life. Dave said that then they can look at the census records and if she was in the same house as Howard on one of the nights of the census then we'll have his surname. Yay.'

'But, Tash,' I said, 'even though this is all fascinating, it doesn't really tell us anything. I could pick a

name randomly from the ethers or a name off a grave-
stone, an old-fashioned-sounding name like . . . Alice
Marshfield or Violet Porter or something, and I bet
you if you looked long enough, you'd find someone
with that name in the records. The fact that Dave's
uncle found a Henrietta Gleeson, so what?'

'Who's Alice Marshfield? Is she another of your
past lives?' asked Tash.

Effy playfully thumped her but ignored her question. 'It might all lead to Howard,' she said to me.

'Yes but even if we found someone called Howard
and he lived in the same place as Henrietta, again, so
what? They might have been neighbours of Betty's
gran and she remembered their names.'

Effy folded her arms. 'I'm not giving up,' she said.

'Me neither,' said Tash. 'And we should call you
"Jo Yes But" from now on because that's what you
keep saying: yes but, yes but.'

'Yes but— I mean, look, I don't want to be a killjoy but I don't want you or Dave wasting your time.
We've got a lot of studying to do this year, let's
focus on that because at least that will help up in
this life.'

'Now you are being a killjoy,' said Tash. 'This is way
more fun than homework.'

'Not to me,' I said. 'It's not going to wash as an excuse if we get low grades, like, sorry, Miss, I was researching a person I was in a past life.'

'OK, then look at it this way,' said Tash. 'You do the research for the magazine, and write a good article because that *will* help towards your CV, and Effy, me and the boys will do the Henrietta stuff. Deal?'

I couldn't argue with that. 'Deal.' Usually the students asked to write articles for *Chillaxin* were in the Upper Sixth whilst team members in the Lower Sixth, like Effy and me, did the groundwork like research and finding sources. But Finn had said I could write it up. It really was too good an opportunity to turn down.

Chapter Nine

'OK, there are two to see this morning and two this afternoon,' I said as I glanced down the printed sheet of names from Finn. 'Want to split up or go together?'

Finn hadn't wasted any time and had already emailed a list of assorted clairvoyants that he managed to get to see Effy and me at short notice. He'd also picked them because they didn't charge a fixed fee but took donations instead. He said he would reimburse us from the *Chillaxin* kitty when we'd finished.

Now it was Saturday and Effy and I had just met in west Hampstead for a quick cappuccino before we headed out to the sessions we were booked in with. It was a sunny day and Effy had a short blue dress on and her turquoise sneakers and I was wearing a black lace vintage top that I'd got from Notting Hill market with my black jeans.

'Let's go together,' said Effy as she spooned froth from her coffee into her mouth. 'We might remember different things.'

I laughed. Effy's nobody's fool. She knew we'd take a different angle on it all. I didn't mind that. I knew it was good journalism to represent different viewpoints.

'It would be amazing if any of them come out with the same story,' Effy continued. 'You know, say that you were Henrietta once.'

'Yes, that *would* be amazing,' I said. 'But it's not going to happen. So. Who's first?'

Effy glanced at our sheet of appointments. 'Annie Simmons. According to her ad in the back of the local paper, the spirits speak to her.'

'What if she evokes someone we don't want and it follows us home?' I asked. 'Like a bad spirit, wuhoohoo.'

'That won't happen,' said Effy, but she said it rather quickly.

I picked up the list and glanced over it again. Number one: Annie Simmons in West Hampstead. Number two: Heather Mason in Kilburn. Number

Three: a group who meet in a church with guest clair-voyants and the last was late afternoon in Muswell Hill. 'Doesn't sound like an awe-inspiring bunch,' I said. 'I hope we get something we can write about.'

'That's because you're not open-minded,' said Effy.

Being accused of not having an open mind by Effy or anyone really bugs me. Effy particularly because she's my mate and supposed to get me, but sometimes she just doesn't. 'There's a difference between being open-minded and gullible.'

Effy bristled. She doesn't like it when I insinuate that she's naïve. I suppose that makes her feel like I don't get *her*. 'I am not gullible. I can spot a fake as well as the next person,' she objected. 'Come on, let's not argue. Let's go and get started. Is Ben coming to any of them to take photos?'

I shook my head. Finn had sent me Ben's email address so we could discuss the article, and I'd sent him our list of appointments, but he'd emailed back saying he preferred to work alone and would go round later to take his pictures. *Miserable git*, I thought, although part of me was glad he wasn't coming along. I didn't know what was going to happen or what was going to be said and I didn't want any witnesses apart from Effy.

'What does your mum think of you doing this research?' asked Effy.

I shrugged. 'Haven't told her. You know what she's like. She'd be here doing it with us. I just said I was working on a magazine article. What about you? You told yours?'

Effy shook her head. 'Same as you. Just said I'm doing stuff for the school magazine. You know *my* mum. She'd put such a dampener on it – bit like you.'

'Sorry, Ef. No more fighting today.'

'Agreed,' said Effy, then grinned. 'As long as you admit that I am right, always was right and always will be.'

'Yes, Your Majestic Queen of bossiness. I hear and obey.'

Effy laughed. 'I supposed it would be boring if we agreed on everything,' she said as my phone bleeped that I had a text. It was from Owen again. **Have a spooktacular time**, he'd written.

'You've been filling Owen in on what we're up to though I see,' I said.

Effy shrugged. 'He always asks after you when he calls home,' she said.

As we left the café and headed off on our way to our first appointment, I remembered Finn's last words to me at the Lock: 'Let me know if any of them mention me.' Now that would be worth going along for, as well as a published article going on my CV. Even though I'd told myself that Finn had a girlfriend and was out of my league, I couldn't get his annoying face out of my mind or the fact that he'd told me that he hadn't met the right girl yet. *Things change*, I thought, *maybe things won't work out with his girlfriend. Maybe that's why he was flirting with me. Maybe already things aren't working out with her. Maybe, maybe, maybe. Yeah right. Maybe I was the one that was gullible.*

It wasn't far to Annie Simmon's house. We rang the bell and a serious young woman with dark scraped-back hair and no make-up answered the door to us. She introduced herself as Faith and led us into a cramped waiting room where a couple of other visitors sat quietly with closed eyes. The place stank of dogs and damp carpets. As I sat down and looked around, I saw that there wasn't a square inch that didn't have some kind of china nick-nack on it: tiny ladies in crinolines, ballet dancers, cats, cute dogs with big sad eyes. The chairs were covered in knitted patchworks and on the wall were pictures of Jesus, the

Sacred Heart. All the clutter combined with the smell made me feel suffocated. After five minutes, Faith called us to follow her to a room at the back where Mrs Simmons was waiting. She looked sweet, like your favourite granny: white hair in a tidy bun, twinkling blue eyes and fluffy rabbit slippers on her feet. She smiled at us and indicated that we should sit on the faded chairs opposite her. Effy's seat was taken by an old-looking cocker spaniel but he got down and proceeded to have a good sniff of our shoes.

'How can I help?' asked Annie.

Effy and I glanced at each other.

'This is Jo,' Effy blurted before I could say anything. 'We, that is she, wanted to know about her past lives.'

Annie beckoned me forward to sit closer to her. She took my hands and closed her eyes for what felt like an eternity. In the meantime, the dog wrapped its front paws around my leg and began to hump my calf. I couldn't push him off because Annie had my hands so I tried a gentle kick but he wouldn't go. I looked over at Effy. 'Help,' I mouthed.

She got up and tried to pull the dog off me. He finally got down and gave Effy the filthiest look before collapsing on her feet when she sat back down. I could see she was trying hard not to laugh.

Finally Annie opened her eyes. 'I see many lives,' she said. 'I see you as a Maasai warrior in deepest Africa. Then a nun in Russia. After that a lady in Japan. Then ancient Egypt. You were a high priestess in the temple. Well respected.' She smiled at me.

'And her last life?' Effy asked.

Annie paused for a moment, took my hands and closed her eyes again. 'Oh. Now this one is interesting.'

Effy and I exchanged glances as Annie began to speak. 'In your last life, you weren't on this planet, dear. You were on a planet called Kinadas in a far-off galaxy.'

I glanced back at Effy. Even she had the decency to roll her eyes.

Annie opened her eyes. 'Anything else I can help you with?' she asked. 'A cup of tea before you go? Faith could fix you one with a nice piece of Battenburg cake.'

'No, thank you. We . . . we have somewhere to go,' I replied.

Annie smiled again. 'You both have lovely souls,' she said. 'Be happy.'

'Thank you,' Effy and I chorused then we headed for the door outside of which Faith was waiting.

'Do you need to sit quietly for a while?' she asked in a hushed voice.

We both shook our heads. 'No, fine, thanks,' I said.

Faith looked disappointed and led us back to the front door.

'Weird,' said Effy as we headed off down the street.

'*Pee wee oink,*' I said in a high-pitched voice.

Effy looked at me as if I was mad.

'That was me being my alien past life self,' I explained. 'Do you not speak extraterrestrial? Now. Who's next on the list?'

'Heather Mason,' she replied.

'Lead the way,' I said. I was beginning to enjoy myself. A few more like Annie and even Effy would have to come around to my way of thinking.

Heather's house was on a quiet street in Kilburn. Inside, it was the total opposite to Mrs Simmons's: white and minimal in style apart from shelves that were full of crystals of every size and colour. A pretty, blonde woman in her twenties let us in. She had huge, pale blue eyes which were slightly glazed, long blonde dreadlocks, tattoos up her arms and was dressed in white with a feather garland around her neck.

'Heather Mason?' asked Effy.

The woman shook her head. 'I was. Now I'm Wind Dancer. My spirit guide gave me the name,' she said without the glimmer of a smile then she led us into her 'treatment room'.

I felt slightly panicked by her. She was well intense. 'But I didn't come for a treatment,' I said when I saw a couch in the centre of the white room. 'Er, Effy, how about you go this time?'

Wind Dancer indicated that Effy should lie on the couch so I sat on a chair in the corner whilst Effy nervously settled herself. 'Er . . . what are you going to do?' she asked.

Wind Dancer picked a peacock feather out of a vase of feathers by the couch. 'Each session is different. We'll see who wishes to come through. Now close your eyes.'

Effy did as she was told. Wind Dancer closed her eyes too and began to wave the feather up and down over Effy, about fifty centimetres away from her body. 'I feel the spirit of Icarus,' she said. 'Speak to us, O master, and heal thy servant.'

Effy opened one eye and when she saw what Wind Dancer was doing, she glanced over at me. I gave her the thumbs up and that set her off. Her shoulders started to shake with silent laughter which set me off and soon both of us were writhing with pain as we tried not to make a noise.

Wind Dancer opened her eyes. 'Be still,' she barked.

'Sorry,' Effy spluttered.

Wind Dancer looked over at me so I quickly straightened my face and coughed. 'Sorry, something stuck in my throat.'

Wind Dancer sighed heavily and her body seemed to deflate. 'The energy is not right in the room. It happens sometimes.'

Effy was off the couch in a flash. 'No worries, Wind Dancer. Thanks for your time.'

We left a ten pound donation and were out the door as fast as we could go although Wind Dancer came after us into the hall where she tried to sell us some of her organic bath products. 'They contain essence of night ray which was captured when the moon was aligned with Venus on the summer solstice.'

'No thanks, Wind Dancer,' Effy said. 'We've got no more money.'

Wind Dancer closed the door on us fast.

'She was spooky,' I said when we reached the corner of the street.

'You weren't the one on the couch,' said Effy and she put up her arms as though they were wings then proceeded to mock-fly down the road. 'I am Icarus.'

An old lady out walking her dog gave her a filthy look then hurried off in the opposite direction.

So far it had been an interesting morning and no mention of Henrietta, Howard or Finn.

In the afternoon – after a quick lunch of basil, mozzarella and tomato ciabatta, yum – we went to the meeting at the local church hall. By the time we got there, the hall was half full of people, mainly elderly. We snuck into the back row trying not to make any noise, but everyone turned around to see who'd come in just the same.

On the stage, a bald, middle-aged man in a black suit was speaking. The trousers to the suit were a tad too short for him and revealed his red socks. He cocked his head up to the right as if listening to someone much in the same way that Betty had when I'd seen her in the tent on the Heath. 'I've got an Annie here,' said the man. 'Anyone here know an Annie?' He looked around at the audience but there were no takers.

'Unless the Annie we saw this morning just passed away,' Effy whispered.

The man listened again to whatever he could see up to his right. 'OK. A Norman. Anyone here know a Norman?' Again, there was no response from the hall. The man sighed. 'OK, someone else is coming through. John. A John. Anyone here know a John?'

To our left, a lady gasped and put up her hand.

'Chances are everyone's got a dead relative called John,' I whispered to Effy.

'John says to tell you that he's fine,' said the man and the lady's eyes filled with tears.

The rest of the meeting went on the same way with the man trying names until he struck lucky with the audience. The message was always the same. 'I'm fine,' the unseen presences would say and it appeared to keep the audience happy. For a split second, I wondered what I'd do if suddenly the man on the stage said that a Robert had come to talk. That was my dad's name. I think my eyes would have filled with tears too even if I didn't believe any of it. However, no Robert put in an appearance invisibly or otherwise that day and despite my cynicism, there was a part of me that wished he had.

After half an hour, Effy whispered, 'Let's get out of here.'

I nodded and we snuck out the back as quietly as we could.

'OK. So that was a waste of time,' said Effy then looked at me. 'And don't say, I told you so.'

'I wasn't going to,' I said, but I couldn't help but feel a sense of relief. Maybe this research would put an end to Effy's obsession with Henrietta. Hopefully we could return to our normal life, homework, boys, hanging out. We stood outside the church hall for a few minutes and got out our phones to do a text check.

'Finn,' I said as I read my text.

'Mark,' said Effy as she read hers. 'Wants to know when I'm going to be finished. What did Finn say?'

'He wanted to know if any of the clairvoyants had mentioned him,' I said as I quickly texted a reply to him. 'I've just told him that everything isn't always about him.'

Effy laughed. My phone beeped again showing another message from Finn, no words this time, just a sad face.

I linked arms with Effy and steered her towards a café. 'You know what? The spirits are telling me, we need hot chocolate. Extra cream.'

'OK. I think you're right,' she said and stuck her arms out à la zombie and began to stagger towards the café on the Kilburn High Road. I joined in too. The old lady with the dog who we'd passed earlier in the day just happened to be passing again. She took one look at us and crossed the road muttering something about, 'Teenagers. Should all be locked up.'

Chapter Ten

Our appointment in Muswell Hill was at five o'clock and Effy and I were there on the dot. The house was a shabby semi-detached that looked badly in need of a new coat of paint. The front garden was overgrown with weeds and littered with an old shopping trolley and bins.

An elderly, unshaven man in a grey tracksuit opened the door, grunted at us and then ushered us into a front room where he left us. It reeked of cigarettes.

We sat down and looked around. A black cat on the faded brown sofa raised an inquisitive eye then fell back asleep. A moment later, a women in her late fifties entered. She was wearing a tracksuit similar to the man's, only hers was maroon. I presumed that she must be Lily, the clairvoyant with whom we had the booking.

She jerked her chin at us. 'Which one?' she asked.

'Your turn,' said Effy.

I stood up. 'Oh hi, I'm Jo.'

Effy stood up too.

'You stay here,' the woman said firmly to Effy. 'Jo, come with me.'

Effy shrugged and sat back down. *Not big on friendliness*, I thought as I followed the woman. She was strange-looking. Everything about her face seemed to be exaggerated: huge eyes, a mass of grey wiry hair that framed her very thin, heavily-lined face. She looked as if she'd put her fingers in an electric socket and got a shock. I was glad she hadn't been our first port of call or I might not have got through the day.

She led me through to a small living room at the back where Lily sat on a hard chair in the corner and lit a cigarette. She pointed at my wrist.

'Your watch,' she said.

I took it off and gave it to her. She pointed to a chair similar to hers next to a table with paper and pencils. 'Sit and write down what I say,' she instructed. 'It might not make sense now but may later.'

I took a piece of paper and waited.

She looked away from me and seemed to be listening to someone up to her right, much in the same way that Betty had when I saw her on the Heath and the bald man had in the church hall earlier. She began to speak. 'Anandpana says someone is here. A man. Says you're wearing his ring.' She pointed to my right hand. 'He died eight years ago. He had difficulty breathing. He died because of his heart.'

I felt shocked by how specific she was and sudden tears filled my eyes. Dad died eight years ago of a heart attack. Mum gave me his wedding ring when I was eleven. I've worn it on my right hand ever since.

'There's a dog with him,' Lily continued.

Rex. Dad's dog died the week after him. I felt stunned. How could she know this?

'He says he is happy and you should be happy also. Don't be afraid. Anandpana says you have been unhappy in love. You don't let yourself love but recently there is a boy. You have known him before. You are meant for each other but there will be obstacles.'

'Who's Anandpana?'

'My spirit guide,' Lily replied.

'Does he, Anandpana, say who this boy is? His name? Um, how recent is recent?' Owen flashed into my mind. I'd known him most of my life. Did recent mean I could rule him out? Lately, his texts had made me laugh and seeing him on the bank holiday a couple of weeks ago had reminded me of how well we got on. If I was honest with myself, I had missed him and our conversations since he'd gone off to uni.

Lily listened up to her right again. 'Time is different on the plane on which Anandpana dwells. He says you will know him. He is a good soul.'

'Can't he give me a name?' I asked. It seemed to me that if Anandpana or Lily could pick up on so much then why couldn't they give a name?

Lily turned her attention to me. It felt like she was looking straight into me and made me feel very uncomfortable. 'He *says* you will know him. Write that down. I have no name. Anandpana says all will be resolved in time.'

Lily was back listening. 'Your friend's cat has gone missing but don't worry, she will return. Someone, maybe your mother, works long hours and needs a break.' *Well at least that last part is true but then probably everybody's mother works too hard*, I thought. Lily stopped and looked at me again. 'Is there anything else you want to ask?'

'Er . . . do you do past life readings? Who I was—'

Lily sighed wearily. 'People always come to me with this kind of question. Often they want to hear they were some glamorous character from history. To escape from the reality of this life into a fantasy in their head. Do you want to hear that you were Cleopatra?'

I shook my head. 'Not especially.'

'Good. So get on with this life. I believe people should move on, not be looking backwards. Life is what you make it this time.'

I nodded, but she was off again as if someone had switched her on.

'Anandpana says that in this life you are here to learn balance. People have many lives, not just one. You have had many. Some lives steeped in your senses, seeking pleasure, some as a recluse seeking answers. In your most recent past life you were a governess, here in England. But you didn't find balance in that life either. Anandpana says that your lesson is this: if you seek pleasure exclusively, you lose the meaning of life, but if you seek the meaning of life exclusively, you lose the pleasure. Only when pleasure and meaning are balanced, will you find true joy.' She looked across at me. 'Anything else?'

'A governess in my last life?' I asked as I scribbled madly, trying to get it all down but at the same time not miss what she was saying.

'Yes. That is when you were with your soulmate. With him, but not with him. You will find him again in this life. Or he will find you.'

'Do you have the name of the governess?' I asked. *Maybe they teach all clairvoyants at psychic school to come out with the same story, I thought. Governess. Soulmate. Lost love. But if she gave the name Henrietta that would be more convincing.*

'No name,' said Lily. 'I don't always get a name.'

'And how will I know who my soulmate is?'

Lily seemed to suddenly tire. 'Why are you here? What do you want?' Her grey eyes pierced into me. I found I couldn't lie.

'I . . . I'm doing research for an article about clair-voyants for a magazine—'

Her expression turned to sadness. 'That is not why you're here. You are here to know the joy of love. To lose your fear. Trust in your destiny. Trust in your heart.'

She handed me back my watch, stood up and opened the door for me to leave.

Meeting over.

I handed over a ten pound note then went back in to join Effy. I felt in a daze. I had a hundred questions I wanted to ask but an elderly lady was waiting to see Lily, and Effy and I were quickly ushered out by the grumpy man.

'How did it go?' asked Effy when we got back onto the street and went through our usual ritual of checking for texts. 'Another waste of time?'

'Not sure,' I answered as I looked on my phone but there were no messages. 'She said that—'

'Oh *no*!' Effy exclaimed as she looked at her messages.

'What?'

'Tash. Cassie's gone missing since this morning. She wants to know if we can go round and help look for her. I'd better let Mark know I can't meet him.'

'No way!' Cassie is Tash's cat, a big, dopey white creature who hardly ever moves from the sofa and certainly never leaves the house. 'Text her back and tell her not to worry. She'll turn up.'

'Jo! This is *Cassie*. You know how much Tash loves that cat. We can't just tell her to chill.'

'I can. Cassie will turn up.'

Effy sighed with exasperation. 'You can't know that.'

'I can. Lily just told me.'

'*Lily* just told you? So suddenly you believe in what clairvoyants tell you? Can you be sure it was about Cassie? What did she say exactly?'

'I—' Effy was right. I couldn't be totally sure but Lily had been spot on about a friend's cat going missing so maybe she was spot on about her reappearing too.

Effy's phone bleeped again before I got a chance to tell her what Lily had said. 'Tash again,' she said as she read her message then sighed with relief. 'Phew. Drama over. They found her in the laundry cupboard.' She put her phone away. 'You were right. So what exactly did Lily say?'

'Just that a mate's cat had gone missing and would show up.'

'Did she say anything else?'

I shrugged. 'I can't remember everything. Some of it was a bit vague like about my mum working too hard.' I decided not to elaborate on the other stuff that Lily had said, the things about my dad and Rex, my ring, and especially not the bit about me having been a governess and how I had to find my soulmate.

Now that Cassie had gone missing then turned up, it was all beginning to feel a bit spooky and I needed time to think. 'But, Effy, whatever Lily was, she was certainly no fake.'

Effy nodded. Luckily she didn't press me further because there was another text from Mark and Effy's attention was elsewhere.

Chapter Eleven

After Effy had gone off, I headed straight home where I let myself in and headed for the kitchen. Sometimes I wished that we had a cat, just so there was somebody living to greet me on evenings like this when Mum was out with a friend and the house felt so quiet. Not that I begrudged Mum a night out, no way. I knew that she needed some fun time as much as anyone, but in the past when she was out I didn't feel being alone as acutely because Tash and Effy were always here with a DVD or ready for a sleepover or I was over at theirs. So much had changed since Dave and Mark had come on the scene. A cat would be the perfect solution. A presence that would be there but not ask too many questions. 'Purrfect solution,' I said out loud.

Mum had left me some chicken in the oven but I didn't feel like eating much. I made myself a hot chocolate and sat at the kitchen table. I pulled out my phone in the hope that there might be more texts. Nothing. I went up to my room to my computer. No emails so I went to Facebook to see what was happening on there. Effy, Tash and I used to use it a lot last year but none of us bother with it that much any more. I went to my page. One message, one request to add a friend and a notification that Owen had poked me. I clicked on the request link to see who it was from. Ohmigod! Finn O'Brady. I immediately clicked confirm. My Saturday evening suddenly got a whole lot more interesting as I accessed his page and began to read his status updates, comments left and checked out his photos. He had thousands of friends, far too many to go through and mainly girls. There were also loads of messages on his wall from girls and probably a ton more private ones I couldn't access. Looking through his photos only confirmed what I was feeling deep inside – that Finn was one hundred per cent gorgeous.

After a short while, a notification on the right of Finn's page attracted my attention. A mini music festival was being held the next afternoon down at Highbury Fields in Islington and Minted were one of the bands playing. Effy and Tash already had plans to go to a movie with Dave and Mark. *What are my options?* I asked myself. *Home alone? Miss Tagalong with my mates or be a free, independent spirit and go to the music festival and see Finn? Hmm? I wonder. . .*

The following day, I woke up late to find that Mum was also still in bed. *Shall I go to the music festival on my own?* I asked myself as I stared outside at the bright sunshine. It seemed a shame to stay inside on such a lovely day and I felt determined to prove to myself that I could still have a good time as a singleton. *I don't need to be with mates or in a couple to get out there,* I told myself. *Life is what you make it.*

I spent a relaxing hour doing a DIY pampering session. First I sang my head off in a honeysuckle bubble bath. After that, I applied my Miss Dior Cherie body lotion then got dressed in my black jeans and a grey tailored silk jacket that had the vintage feel that I like. A touch of make-up (I didn't want to look as if I'd tried too hard), then I blow-dried my hair until it shone.

Mum was up by the time I went downstairs and looked up from the Sunday papers. 'Wow, you look lovely,' she said. 'Going somewhere special?'

'Music festival,' I muttered. 'Back in a few hours.'

'Take your phone,' she called as I let myself out the front door.

The park was already full by the time I got to Highbury Fields, with people seated on the ground near the front, others chatting or standing and listening at the back, a few lying flat out on their backs enjoying the sunshine. I went to stand under a tree and scanned the crowds. I felt slightly wobbly being on my own and for a few moments wished that Effy or Tash was there with me. It would have been more fun to have someone to chat to. *No. I am OK*, I told myself. *I am an independent spirit*.

I listened to a couple of bands then went to get a drink from a stall at the back of the park. As I stood in the queue, a group of older boys came and stood behind me. They stank of alcohol. One of the boys had a cigarette in his hand. 'Got a light?' he asked.

'Don't smoke,' I said.

'You look smoking to me, babe,' said his dark-haired friend. The others cracked up as if he'd said the funniest thing ever.

'Here on your own, are you?' the first boy persisted.

'Um . . . with some mates,' I replied.

He looked around. 'I can't see them,' he said.

'We could be your mates,' said his friend and they stepped nearer to me as if closing in.

I tried to step away but they moved with me and were so drunk that they were swaying on their feet. I felt myself being shoved towards an area behind the drinks van where there were tall bins spilling over with cans and uneaten bits of pizza and bread. I felt my breath shorten. *Keep cool*, I told myself but inside, I was starting to panic.

Behind them, I suddenly noticed Finn and a very tall, well-built black man with a shaved head walking past. Luckily, Finn glanced in my direction and saw me. He nudged the man he was with. He clocked the situation straight away and came striding over with Finn.

'Hey, Jo, there you are,' said Finn. 'We've been looking for you everywhere. Come on.' He came and put his arm around me and led me away.

His companion nodded at the boys. 'All right, lads?' he asked.

One of them muttered something and they dispersed quickly, almost tripping over a bin as they went.

'You OK?' asked Finn.

I nodded. 'Yes, thanks. They were drunk, I think.'

'There are always a few idiots at events like this,' he said. He glanced around. 'You on your own?'

'No . . . actually . . . yes,' I said.

'No, yes?' He got that amused look in his eye again.

'OK. Yes. On my own.'

'So come and join us. We have a camper over there,' he said and he pointed to an area to the back of the stage. 'That is if you want to.'

'I want to,' I said. I didn't want any more encounters with drunk boys.

'Cool.' Finn indicated the black man who was walking with us. 'And this is Roger. Looks after us at events like this.'

'Hi, Roger,' I said.

We walked over to the camper van and as we got closer, I saw that there was a group of girls hanging about outside and a serious-looking security man standing guard at the bottom of the steps. He nodded at Finn.

Finn nodded back and pointed at me. 'She's with me,' he said. A groan of disappointment came from the girls as we swept past them and into the van. It felt brilliant! *First he's my hero coming to my rescue*, I thought, *and now I'm part of his entourage. It doesn't get any better than this*. At the thought of his entourage, I suddenly remembered the girl with auburn hair. Would she be around? I'd have loved to ask him who she was and what she was to him but even I'm not so dumb as to ask a boy questions like that so early on.

There was no sign of her inside the van and after making sure I got a seat and a drink, Finn's attention was soon on getting ready for the gig. Ben came in at one point and did a double take when he saw me sitting near Finn and chatting to him. He turned around and went straight out again.

'What's with Ben?' I asked.

Finn glanced at the door. 'Nothing. He's probably gone to walk his dog or gone to check the sound on stage or something. Why?'

'Oh nothing,' I said. It seemed a rational enough explanation but I got the feeling that he'd left because he'd seen me there. *He doesn't even know you*, I told myself. *You're imagining things*.

The rest of the afternoon was a blast. Finn insisted I stick with the band and sit on the side of the stage to watch their set. All the other boys in the band were a real laugh and I felt totally in with the in-crowd. The only one who was aloof was Ben who still acted as though I didn't exist. It didn't matter, Finn acted as though I did.

One of the best days of my life, I thought as I sat on the bus going home. First I called the girls to tell them about my day and catch up, then I replayed the events of the afternoon over and over in my mind. Finn putting his arm around me. Saying, 'She's with me.' Checking I was OK in-between songs. Saying, 'Later,' when we finally parted and he had to go off with the rest of the band in the van. *Later*. That meant something, didn't it? Later? A promise of things to come. *Past lives. Who needs to go there when my future is looking so rosy?* I thought as I stared out of the bus window.

Chapter Twelve

On Monday evening, Mum took me for my appointment with my hypnotherapist, Fiona Peters. Mum
stayed in the waiting room whilst I went in to see
Fiona. She's a nice lady, about Mum's age, with kind
hazelnut-coloured eyes and long brown hair – which
I'd love to cut because it makes her look like an old
hippy. She looked up as I entered her room.

'Hi, Jo, take a seat and I'll be right with you.'

As Fiona finished writing something in her desk
book, I glanced around the room. A Turkish rug on
the floor, shelves of books on every type of therapy, a
statue of an Indian goddess and on the walls were her
certificates and various posters. Hypnotherapy for
weight loss, confidence issues, phobias, smoking, fear

of flying. Certificates for hypnotherapy, NLP (whatever that is), cognitive behaviour therapy. There was one in the corner I hadn't noticed before. Past life regression therapy.

'Hey, Fiona, you do past life regression?'

She looked up and nodded. 'Sometimes a trauma goes back a long *long* way.'

'Wow. So you actually believe we have past lives?'

'I do.'

'So how come we've never tried regression as part of my therapy?'

'Because we've been focusing on what's causing your dream. You felt that it was because of memories of your father in this life, so it hasn't felt necessary to look further back than that. Regression isn't for everybody. If it's appropriate, I find that it comes up spontaneously in a session. The unconscious mind tends to throw up what is most useful to us. I never plan it because it's not something that can be forced.'

'Can it happen that you go back and get stuck there, you know, in a past life? Er . . . not that I really believe in them. But what if you were a mad person or . . . or a warthog and you got stuck in that life?'

Fiona laughed. 'There's no danger of that happening, Jo. In fact, a past life regression is not dissimilar to what we've been doing already in your sessions with me. I put you into a light trance and see where it takes us.'

It was true. Quite often as I dozed off and listened to Fiona's voice, I found myself remembering times from my childhood that I'd completely forgotten about.

'With a past life regression,' Fiona continued, 'we just go back a little further. Why? What's brought on the sudden interest?'

'Oh . . . just recently someone told me that I was a governess named Henrietta in a past life. It got me thinking about whether I believe in that sort of thing.'

'And who was this someone who told you this?'

'A clairvoyant. My mate Effy dragged me along to see her.'

'Ah, I see. Hence the sudden interest in past lives and regression.'

'That and, well, I never noticed the certificate on your wall before,' I said.

Fiona nodded. 'People don't tend to notice things until they become relevant to them. That certificate has been up there ever since you've been coming to see me. So, Jo, tell me. How do feel about what you were told?'

'I think the clairvoyant probably tells the same story to lots of people who go to see her.'

Fiona nodded but didn't say anything. She often did this in sessions as if waiting for me to fill the silence.

'But my mates seem to believe the whole thing.'

'And how do you feel about that, Jo?'

'Mixed. Pressurised to go along with it, like, they think it's so romantic, but the more rational side of me thinks it's nonsense.'

'The more rational side. Ah. So is there another side that's not so rational?'

'No. Maybe. I don't know. I mean it can't be true, can it?'

'Can't it? What do you think?'

I was silent for a minute while I tried to work out what I really thought. 'Hard one that. I'm not sure what I think any more. Er . . . I like to think I'm open-minded but I also think that some people that go to clairvoyants are gullible. I believe what I see.'

'And what do you see?'

'My mates off on one. They're so into it. The clair-voyant said that Henrietta was in love with someone and they were soulmates, so in the same way that I'm back in this life, so is he and I should find him.'

Fiona smiled. 'Makes sense. If reincarnation is to be believed, chances are others from your past lives are back. Souls who were your mother, your father, your partners, your friends.'

'Whoa. Information overload.'

'If you read anything about reincarnation, it often says that souls are reborn in clusters, bound together through time, maybe because they have unfinished business. Your mother might have been your sister in a past life. Your friend might have been your mother.'

'No way!'

'Why not? We don't actually know a lot about where we've come from or how we got here, do we? But haven't you ever had that feeling when you've met someone that they're familiar, like you've met them before but can't place it?'

I nodded. 'I did with Effy. I feel like I've known her forever. First time I saw her in junior school, there was something familiar about her.'

'Maybe she was your brother or sister in another life.'

'Yeah right.' Despite my trying to be more open-minded, the notion that I'd known just about everyone in my life in a past life was taking it all too far. It would seem like too much of a coincidence.

'As I said, Jo, we don't know a lot, do we? And you did say your friend Effy seemed familiar when you met her.'

'OK,' I said, 'but I doubt if she was my brother or sister, more like she would have been my mother. She's so bossy. Always telling me what to do or wear or think.'

Fiona laughed and indicated the couch. 'So. Are you ready to begin our session?'

'Sure.' I got up and moved over to the couch.

'How've you been since the last time we met, Jo?'

'Better actually, apart from one night when I had the same old dream.'

'OK. This time I'd like to work a little deeper with you and see if we can get back to the dream and the feeling behind it.'

'Loss. I always wake with such a sense of loss.'

'That's the feeling we need to explore. What do you feel that loss is?'

I shrugged. 'I always feel fuddled when I wake up. The dream fades so quickly that I can't remember much. I'm pretty sure it's about losing Dad.'

'And is that your rational mind telling you that or another part of you?'

'Oh. Don't know. My gut, I guess, and Mum says she hears me calling for someone and it sounds like Dad.'

'OK. Let's see if we can go from pretty sure that it's about losing your dad to certain. If we can get to the feeling behind the dream, get into that loss and confront it, you'll be able move on. Is there anything else you can remember from the dream?'

'Sometimes there's a house.'

'Is it the house you used to live in when your father was alive?'

'No. It's not a house that I know.'

Fiona nodded. 'Sometimes we dream in symbols. A house can represent yourself – the basement your fears, the attics your dreams and hopes. A closed room may represent a part of you that is closed off. Don't worry about it though. As you relax, it may become clearer what it means. OK. Ready?'

I lay down, but my mind had gone into a spin. *Two different people had told me about me being a governess. Should I ask if we can give the past life regression a go to see if there is actually anything to it?* I wondered. *Plus it would show Effy and Tash just how open-minded I can be and it would be amazing if I actually experienced anything.*

'Er . . . Fiona. Do you think we could try a past life regression today?' I asked. 'It might help answer some questions for me.'

Fiona regarded me for a few moments. 'We can see where this session takes us but as I said, it only happens if it's going to be useful – if the time is right. But we can see how far back your unconscious is willing to take you if you wish.' She got up and went towards the door. 'I want to check with your mum that she's happy if we do this. OK?'

'Sure,' I replied. I was certain Mum wouldn't object, in fact she'd probably want to have a go herself when she heard that Fiona did regressions. Like Effy, it was the sort of thing she'd be well into, and indeed, Fiona was back a few minutes later.

'She says whatever might help,' she said.

'Can you bring me back at any point if I don't like it?' I asked. I felt nervous but also excited to be trying something different. Although Tash and Effy tease me about being a cynic, it's not that. I like hard facts. Evidence. That's why I like science. I enjoy the research of it. Proving a hypothesis. A past life regression could be an interesting experiment but it also felt like a leap into the unknown.

Fiona nodded. 'Nothing can happen without you wanting it to happen. You'll be in control all the time just like our other sessions.'

I'll probably fall asleep as always, I thought as I settled down.

'I'd like to record the session if that's OK with you,' said Fiona. 'Partly for research purposes and partly because, depending on what comes up, clients find it useful to listen to what has gone on when they are in trance.'

'Fine by me,' I said.

Fiona found the recording equipment then sat on a chair beside me and told me to close my eyes. 'Let's start by focusing on your recurring dream and not try to force the regression but we'll see where the session takes us. Is that OK?'

I nodded and she began to talk me through the usual countdown. I found it soothing to listen to her soft voice as she asked me to concentrate on my breathing and, after a few minutes, I began to feel myself relaxing. I trusted her not only because of her manner but also because Mum had thoroughly looked into her training before she let me see her. 'I don't want you seeing a whack job,' Mum'd said when she'd first suggested the sessions. 'Or one of these people who do a weekend course then set themselves up as practitioners and start playing with people's minds without the proper training or experience.'

'Good, very good,' Fiona said. 'Keep focusing on your breath, Jo, six, starting to feel very peaceful, five, your body growing heavy, four, your breathing is slow and easy and free, three, you're safe and warm, two, relaxed, floating . . .'

I was vaguely aware of Fiona's voice droning on in the background. I felt as if I was falling asleep and she instructed me to imagine that I was in a lift, going down, down, down. 'The lift door opens, you see steps, going down. You start to go down them, down, down . . . completely at ease. Now I want you to go back to a time when the dream first started, but only if it feels right. If it feels safe to do so. It might be this life, might be a past one. Tell me, Jo, what do you see?'

I shook my head. I couldn't see anything. It was misty. Was I supposed to visualise something apart from steps? My mind felt foggy.

'Where are you, Jo?'

'I don't know,' I replied. *I'm here on your couch in the clinic in Highgate*, said my mind but I didn't feel like I had the energy to say that. My body felt heavy, so relaxed. I followed Fiona's voice as she told me to go down more steps, '. . . down, down, down . . . Feeling safe. Feeling relaxed.'

119

'Where are you, Jo?' Fiona asked again sometime later. 'What do you see?'

The mist began to clear inside my head. I had the sense of being in a crowd.

'A street,' I said.

'Who's looking at the street? Is it you?'

'Don't know.'

'Does this person have a name?'

Somewhere in my brain, I felt uncomfortable and I felt myself stir out of the pleasant reverie I'd been in. 'I'm sorry, Fiona, but I feel like I want to say Henrietta because I've been told about her. Like I want to relax, but might be trying to make something happen by thinking of her.'

'Lie back. Keep focusing on your breath, Jo. Relax. Let it all go. Don't force anything. You don't have to do a thing or make anything happen. If it's right that you go back to a certain time, it's going to happen, it will. Trust your unconscious mind, it is your friend. Let go, relax.'

As I continued to listen to her voice, I let myself drift off again, relieved that I didn't have to think about past lives or Henrietta or what Effy or Tash thought of me. I felt so tired.

'Keep breathing, Jo. Let yourself go wherever feels

right. Breathe in and out. Relaxed. Feeling calm. Moving down. . .'

I was vaguely aware that Fiona was talking about another lift going down to other levels. *Blimey, I must be way underground by now*, I thought as I followed her instructions and fell back into the peaceful doze.

'. . . warm and comfortable. Where are you now, Jo?'

In my head, I felt as if I was watching a film. My life streaming backwards. Images I knew so well. Doing a DIY makeover with Effy. Laughing our heads off because we both looked like ghouls. A bicycle in the hall. My bicycle. Our dog, Rex, out on the lawn when I was in a paddling pool. Earlier. Dad getting into a car, waving him off to work with Mum. Further back. Mum in the kitchen cooking Sunday lunch. I could smell the roast chicken and onions for the gravy. Further back. I felt so small, so young. Mum and Dad's faces looking down at me while I'm lying in a cot. Then a mist but it feels nice, like floating on clouds. The clouds clear. I'm looking down and see a young, dark-haired woman lying on a bed in a small room. Bent over her is a man with dark hair, though I can't see his face. I can't tell his age but he's not old. I feel a jolt and suddenly I sense that *I* am the woman and the man is holding *my* hand. I still can't see his face because he is turned away.

'Where are you, Jo?' Fiona asked again.

'Room.'

'Who's looking at the room?'

'Not sure. Me, but not me. I have my eyes closed but I can see.'

'Are you all right there, Jo?'

I nod but I sense that the man is distressed. He squeezes my hand and says, 'I will find you. I will find you.'

I don't feel upset. I have the sensation of moving, being pulled up and out of the young woman's body, and again, I am looking down on her from above. She looks serene, the man still holding her hand, bent over her. I feel as if I am moving through a dark tunnel but it isn't frightening. It feels good. I begin to move faster through circles of light. I feel so at home in this light and continue through the most fantastic firework display of gold and white. It is so beautiful and I feel myself melting into it as if becoming one with it.

'Jo, *JO*. Where are you? Focus on your breathing. You're coming back now. Safe, warm, relaxed. Feel the couch beneath you. Become aware of the distant traffic sounds outside the clinic. Safe, warm, relaxed.

When I count down from five, you will awaken, five . . . four. . .'

I didn't want to awaken. I wanted to stay where I was. It felt so peaceful there. But I could feel my body starting to stir. It felt heavy after being in the light.

'Three . . . two . . . one and back in the room.'

I opened my eyes.

'How do you feel, Jo?' Fiona asked.

I took a deep breath. I felt like I'd had the most fantastic deep sleep and was totally refreshed and recharged. 'Absolutely blooming wonderful!' I said and grinned. 'How long was I under? It felt like about ten minutes.'

Fiona checked her watch. 'About an hour.'

Chapter Thirteen

Mum was straight in with the interrogation about my session as soon as we got into the car. She assumed that my reason for wanting to try regression was to help with my insomnia so I didn't tell her much apart from the fact that I felt great. She was always trying to get me to open up to her but I never did, not any more, not since Dad died.

I certainly wasn't ready to talk about the Henrietta story with her. With Effy and Tash, even though they were into it, I could still treat it like a bit of fun, but if I talked to Mum, somehow it would feel more solid, with more of a possibility of being real. Plus I needed home to be a space that was Henrietta free.

'I just felt totally relaxed, Mum,' I told her. 'Yes, images were floating about in my head from my child-hood, like photographs I'd forgotten about, but mainly it just felt floaty, nice.'

'Did it give some insight as to why you keep having your recurring dream?' she asked.

I shook my head. 'Not really.'

'So what happened? Did you go back to another country? A time in history? I've always been drawn to Egypt, to the music and the dance. Didn't you discover you were Cleopatra or someone like that?' asked Mum as she pulled out of the car park.

'No, Mum.' That much was true.

I might not have been up for telling Mum the full story, but I did tell the girls. I filled them in on the session on the bus to school the next morning.

'Who do you think the people were that you saw?' asked Tash.

'I don't know,' I said. 'All I do know is that last night I had the best night's sleep I've had in years.'

'I think they were Howard and Henrietta,' said Effy.

'You would,' I said. 'But what I saw could so easily be an image from a film I saw once or even an image

125

I conjured up myself because we've been talking and thinking about past lives for the last few weeks. Maybe I fell so deeply asleep that I was dreaming. In fact, I think that's exactly what happened.'

Effy nodded. 'Maybe, but what came after that, going through a tunnel and into light, that sounds exactly how people describe near-death experiences.'

'Near death? I think that's a bit dramatic, Effy. I was fine. I was lying on a couch in Highgate totally alive. I often see light in my head when I'm going off to sleep, just not that intense before.'

'I'll lend you one of my dad's books,' said Effy. 'It's called *Life After Life*.' She grinned. 'You'll like it, it's a *scientific* study of people who have experienced clinical death.'

'What does that mean?' asked Tash.

'That technically they died on the operating table or in an accident or something, their heart stopped but they were revived to tell the tale.'

'I was hypnotised, not having a clinical death on an operating table or having an accident. I was safe. I was *fine*.'

'Yes but what you experienced sounds the same. I'm not saying *you* were having a death experience but maybe you were reliving Henrietta's.'

'Wow, you have such a vivid imagination, Effy.'

'Just read the book, will you, Jo? What's so amazing about it is that despite people's religious beliefs or faith, the experiences that they recount are similar. All described the light you talked about and also the feeling of well-being and peace.'

'OK, fine,' I said. 'I'll read it if only to keep you happy.' *Remember, remember Owen's wise words, the path of least resistance works best with Effy*, I told myself.

'I love what your hypnotherapist said about souls being born into the same families and circles of friends time after time,' said Effy.

'Unless you have a family you hate,' I said. 'Then you'd want to get well away from them.'

'I guess,' said Tash. 'But maybe that's why you come back with them, to work stuff out, the good and the bad.'

I nodded. 'That's what Fiona said. Unfinished business.'

'I like the idea that we might have known each other before, Jo,' said Effy. 'I had the same feeling that you did when I met you, like, oh there you are. You seemed so familiar.'

I smiled at her, we obviously both felt the same way.

'Hey, what about me?' asked Tash.

Effy regarded her. 'First time on the planet, mate. Jo and I are old souls.'

Tash moved forward to pinch her arm but Effy pulled away. 'Just joking, Tash. You were probably Guinevere or some romantic heroine.'

'Nah, you were a cleaner, I reckon,' I said. 'Or a pig farmer's wife.'

Tash stuck her tongue out. 'Oink to you,' she said.

'Any word from Finn?' Effy asked.

I shook my head. 'He said "Later" when I left him on Sunday, but "later" in boy speak can mean anything from next week to next month.'

Effy and Tash both nodded in agreement.

Our bus arrived at our stop and we got off and headed for the school gates. The effects of the session last night were still with me and I felt well chilled and in such a good mood that even Effy threatening to thrust her near-death book on me couldn't faze me.

After school, I went up to Highgate village with Effy and whilst she dashed home to get her dad's book, I waited for her at her mum's estate agents.

I like Effy's mum and get on with her. Sometimes I wonder if Effy and I were swapped at birth because personality-wise Effy's so much more like my mum and I'm more like hers. Looks-wise there's no confusion though. I'm just like Mum physically, dark with brown eyes, and Effy takes after her mother. Mrs Davis is small and blonde but her dress sense is more classic than Effy's Topshop latest style.

'How's the hunt for Henrietta going?' she asked me. I could tell by the way she arched her right eyebrow that she thought it was all nonsense.

'You know Effy,' I replied.

Her mum sighed. 'I do. She does talk some nonsense sometimes. I don't know where she gets it from. Not from me, I can tell you. I mean it's a sweet story, the governess and her lost soulmate, but anyone with half a brain would know that the clairvoyant made it up.'

'That's what I said.'

'At least Effy has one sensible friend. It sounds like Tash is as taken by the idea as Effy is.'

'Owen advised me to go along with it and that it'll burn out like so many other phases.'

Mrs Davies nodded. 'Sound advice. So he's been in touch with you then?'

I nodded. 'Texts, emails, but we talked about it when he was last back from uni.'

'He keeps a photo of you in his wallet, you know,' she confided. Effy's mum was another one who wanted to see me back with Owen.

I felt myself squirming. I felt bad that I'd broken up with Owen. 'That's nice. It's just, I . . . we . . . we both felt that with him being at uni that we should . . . you know, no ties. He must be meeting loads of new girls there. I didn't want to hold him back.'

'He hasn't met anyone special, I don't think,' said Mrs Davies and she gave me a meaningful look.

Luckily our chat was interrupted by prospective house-hunters. I sighed with relief as the door opened and a couple came in. I never know what to say when Mrs Davis brings Owen up. I can't tell her the truth, like, oh yeah, I like Owen, your son, but he doesn't make my toes curl. Not really what any mother wants to hear!

Effy's mum got up to greet them. 'Hello, can I help you?'

As Mrs Davis attended to the clients, I glanced out of the window. I spotted Ben outside with his dog. He glanced at his watch then looked down the street as if looking for someone. He turned and looked in the window. For once, he wasn't wearing his shades. Our eyes met and for a moment, there was a jolt of recognition. He stared. I stared. No smile.

Oh this is ridiculous, I thought. *I'm going to go and talk to him. Break the ice properly. We have to speak sometime if we're going to be working on the clairvoyant article together.*

I got up and walked out onto the street to join him. 'Hey,' I said. 'I don't think we've actually met properly. I'm Jo Harris—'

'I know who you are,' he said.

Boy, he really is unfriendly, I thought. 'OK. And you're Ben Fraser and don't say you know who you are as well because that would be obvious.'

A glimmer of a smile crossed his face. Without his shades, he was actually quite good-looking. Amber brown eyes, even features and a full wide mouth – if he smiled once in a while, he'd be very attractive – and he had a nice voice, soft but deep. His dog nuzzled my hand so I bent over and gave him a stroke.

'What's his name?' I asked.

'Max,' Ben replied.

'So how do you know me?' I asked.

He looked straight into my eyes. 'You don't remember?'

His gaze was so intense, like he was really looking

into me. It made me feel strange. Exposed in some way. I looked away, leant on one hip and attempted to look unflustered. 'Um . . . Yeah. Course I remember. I saw you playing on the Heath, at the fair and then again at Camden Lock. You're in Minted with Finn, yeah?'

'Finn. Yeah. No, not then.'

'Oh. The *Chillaxin* meetings. My friend Effy said you'd been at them.' I was beginning to feel awkward, bad for not having noticed him.

'Yeah I've seen you at those too. But we met before that.'

'When?'

'At junior school. I remember you.' He stared at me intently again.

I felt myself blush and had to look away. I didn't remember him from school. 'Oh. Sorry. Long time ago I guess.'

He shrugged his shoulder and let out a sigh. 'I guess. Whatever. Ages ago.'

'So as we're going to be working on an article together – the one about clairvoyants – I thought maybe we should talk about it. What angle you're taking and that.'

'What angle are you taking?' he asked.

'Oh. To tell you the truth, I've only made some rough notes so far. I'm not sure what I'm going to write yet. We've seen a few. One seemed genuine, others seemed sincere but no more in touch with the spirit world than me or . . . your dog, Max.'

'Are you into all that stuff?'

'Not really. It's more Effy's thing.'

He nodded.

'What do you think about it all?' I asked.

He rolled his eyes. 'Load of tosh. Fodder for idiots.'

I laughed. 'Don't hold back. Tell me how you really feel.'

That glimmer of a smile again. He'd be cute if he lightened up.

'That's how I feel,' he said. 'What's your opinion?'

'Same as yours. Well, mainly. For gullible people—'

'They tell people what they want to hear. End of.'

'Yes. At least, maybe. I don't know any more.'

'Why? Have you've been told something that's come true?'

'Not exactly. I. . .' I didn't want to tell him about Lily and her pointing to my dad's ring nor did I want to tell him about the Henrietta story. That was private stuff plus I was getting the message fast that Ben was as cynical as me, or at least, as I used to be. Not that

I'd changed my mind that much, but I was definitely wavering around the edges.

'Give me your number,' said Ben. 'When you've thought about the article more and what you really think maybe we can talk.'

I scribbled my number on a piece of paper and gave it to him. He put it in his pocket. He began to walk away then turned back. 'Hey, Jo.'

'Yes.'

He pulled a piece of paper out of his pocket and handed it to me. 'Exhibition next week. Not far from here. It's on at the Highgate Literary and Scientific Institute. Starts next Friday. I've got a few photos in.'

'Oh, right, thanks,' I said. 'Good for you.'

'You haven't seen them yet.'

'No, I haven't. I meant good for you getting work into an exhibition.'

Ben glanced at the leaflet in my hand. 'No obligation but you could see what I do. It's on for a few weeks. If you're interested.'

Effy appeared down the pavement and when Ben saw her, he began to move on. 'OK, bye then,' he said.

'What was that all about?' asked Effy when she joined me.

I glanced after Ben. 'Not sure. He's weird, sort of intense. He's invited us to a photo exhibition.'

'Us or you?' asked Effy.

'Anyone I think. I don't know. He's hard to read. Says he remembers me from junior school. I felt bad I didn't remember him.'

Effy looked down the street at Ben walking away. 'Nice dog though.'

'Yeah,' I said. 'Nice dog, shame about the owner.'

Effy thrust the near-death experiences book into my hand. 'In the meantime, this should keep you busy.'

'Thanks,' I said. As we went back into the agency to join Effy's mum, Ben's face flashed through my mind. The way he looked at me. Interested, but guarded, like he didn't want to give anything away. I made myself think back to junior school. A boy called Ben Fraser. Nope. I couldn't recall him.

Chapter Fourteen

'So who's this Howard then?' asked Mum when I got home later that evening.

'What do you mean?' I asked.

Mum pointed to the answering machine in the hall. 'There's a message for you on there from Tash. She sounded very excited, said they've found Howard. Is he some new boy you've got your eye on?'

'No. Nothing like that.'

'So who is he?'

Hmm. How to explain? Oh Howard, yeah, he's a corpse, as in six foot under. Not what you want to hear about your daughter's latest crush. 'I'll tell you later, Mum. Let me phone Tash.'

I took the phone from the hall and went into our front room to call her. I didn't want Mum listening in and then giving me the third degree.

'Jo, you got my message?' said Tash when she picked up.

'Yes. What have you found?'

'Dave's uncle's been on the case again. It's amazing. You're not going to believe it.'

'Just *tell* me Tash.'

'Oh, right. Yeah. So, Dave was looking into the census records and he found Henrietta and where she lived! Hold on, I've got it written down. Halville House, Trafalgar Road, London. The record said she was governess in the household of a Dr Edward Watts, that he was head of the house, and also there on the night that the census was taken were his wife Lydia Watts and their two boys, wait for it, Howard and Daniel and Lydia's mother, Violet Emery.'

'No way. Oh my God.' I was shocked. I had never really imagined that they had *all* actually existed. And here was proof not just of Henrietta, but a whole family. My rational mind soon kicked in. 'Might not mean anything. As I've said all along, they might have been relatives of Betty's and she was using their names.'

137

'Killjoy,' said Tash. 'Come on, Jo. You have to admit this is interesting at least. Anyway, that's not all. Apparently Dave's been able to dig even further and he's found out that Dr Watts was married, and Daniel and Howard were christened, at St George's church in Highgate—'

'St George's? I know exactly where that is. It's just a bit further down from the square.'

'I know. Amazing, isn't it? We're going to look up Trafalgar Road too in a moment. Imagine if we can find Halville House. You might remember it. And we can go to the church too. Henrietta could have gone to Daniel's christening. Have you ever been inside?'

'No. Never.'

'So you'll come with us?'

Despite all my doubts, I couldn't help but feel a shiver of the excitement that Tash was clearly feeling. 'Yeah. Course but it might not prove anything. So these people existed. It might be a dead end.'

Tash cracked up. 'Dead end. Very funny. So tomorrow after school OK?'

'OK.'

I hung up the phone, still feeling a bit in shock. It felt like the whole thing was building a momentum and I was being taken along with it whether I liked it or not. It would be nice to talk everything over with someone besides Tash and Effy. *Owen*, I thought and pulled out my mobile and dialled his number.

'Hey, what's up?' he said a moment later.

'Tash has found Henrietta, the family she worked for and where they lived.'

'No way!'

'That's what I said. What do you think?' In the background over the phone, I heard someone talking to Owen. 'Oh. Bad time? Sorry, Owen, are you busy?'

'No, it's fine. Just got a mate over for supper.'

'Mate?'

'Susie. She's on the same course as me.'

'Oh. Hey, no matter. I'll call another time, yeah?'

'Yeah,' said Owen, then I heard him laugh at something Susie had said then he hung up. I was surprised to find that I felt jealous. Owen was always there for me. Complete attention. I wasn't sure how I felt about sharing him with another girl.

'Jo, dinner,' Mum called from the kitchen.

'Can I eat later?' I called back.

'No. It's salmon. It will dry out and I want to hear about Howard.'

Reluctantly I went into the kitchen and prepared myself for her questions. There was no point fighting it, when Mum wanted to know about something, she wore away at it until surrender.

Mum sat opposite me. 'Are you OK, Jo?'

I nodded. 'Yes. Fine. Why?'

'Just you seem preoccupied lately. Is anything worrying you?'

'No. Not really.'

'You know you can always talk to me.'

'I know.'

She got up and put our food out on plates. We ate our meals in silence. Suddenly she started to laugh.

'What's so funny?' I asked.

'Oh . . . just hearing Tash mention a Howard earlier.'

'So what's funny about that?'

'It brought back some memories. When you were little, you had an imaginary friend. We were quite worried about you for a while because you talked about him, and to him, non-stop until you were about five. Don't you remember?'

I shook my head.

'You used to insist that he ate at the table with us,' Mum continued, 'and I had to lay a place for him. It was most unlike you because apart from that, you were such a serious, sensible little girl.'

'So what's made you remember all that now?'

'Tash's call. You see, in a world of Sams, Daves and Mikes, you called your friend Howard. Such an old-fashioned name. We wondered where you came up with it.'

I almost choked on my supper.

Chapter Fifteen

As we stood outside St George's church on Wednesday evening after school, I stared up at the tall spire and tried to see if it evoked any memory. It didn't.

'Does it feel familiar?' asked Tash.

I pretended that I was going to faint. 'I . . . oh . . . yes, oo, it's all coming back to me—'

'She's messing about,' said Effy. 'Take no notice of her.'

'Of *course* it's familiar,' I said. 'I've been past here a million times on the way to school but beyond that, no, I can't say it's bringing anything up.'

Effy looked disappointed.

Tash pointed at the door where an elderly-looking vicar with white hair was going in. 'Hey, it's open,' she said and tugged on my arm. 'Let's go in.'

Effy was off in a flash. The decision had been made for me. We *were* going in.

Once inside the dark interior, we could see that the vicar was up near the altar on the left. I gazed around at the pews, the stained glass windows and the chapel. It felt so quiet and peaceful and the smell of frankincense mixed with the fragrance of lilies from the enormous displays filled the air. I breathed in the scent and silence but had no feeling of déjà vu. The only sensation I got was that the altar was on the wrong side. For some reason, when we'd gone in, I'd expected it to be on the right of the door.

The vicar saw us and came towards us. 'Can I help you?'

'I was wondering if you kept records of people buried here? If there was a cemetery at the back of the church—' I started.

'We . . . I've been doing some family research and . . .' said Effy, 'and my great-great-uncle was a parishioner here. I believe that he was married in St George's and might even be buried here. Um . . . do you have any records? It would mean a lot to his family.'

I went red as she lied away, but when she mentioned the part about her great-great-uncle being a parishioner, the vicar looked interested.

'Do you have an idea of when he died?' asked the vicar.

'Oh! Can you remember, Tash?' she asked.

'I think about 1910 or maybe a bit later,' said Tash.

'What was his name?'

'Edward Watts,' Effy replied.

'Watts? Hmmm, I can't be a hundred per cent sure without looking it up, but the adjoining cemetery is small so it's unlikely that he's buried here. The population expanded in the late eighteen hundreds to such an extent that it was too much for the local graveyards. So because of the date it's more likely that he's buried elsewhere. I'm sorry to disappoint you. However, several large cemeteries were plotted to cope with the numbers so you could try Highgate Cemetery down the road, it's much bigger and took the overflow. There are regular tours you could join.'

'Tours around a graveyard?' I asked.

The vicar nodded. 'Highgate Cemetery is famous as are many of the people buried there. Elizabeth Siddal—'

'Dante Rosetti's wife? That Elizabeth Siddal?' I asked. I had a poster of her as Ophelia painted by Millais on my wall as well as one of her as Beatrix painted by Rossetti.

'Indeed,' replied the vicar. 'And Michael Faraday is there too. He invented electricity.'

'But where would we look for Edwards Watts?' said Effy. 'I know the cemetery. It's vast.'

The vicar smiled. 'It's nice to meet youngsters who are so interested in the past. If you can hang on, I can look in the church records to see if his death is recorded and it might also tell us what part of the cemetery he's in.'

'Really?' said Tash. 'Brilliant.'

We followed the vicar to a room at the back of the church, Effy filling him in on the rest of the family and Henrietta as we walked.

In the office were rows and rows of old leather-bound books. The vicar heaved down a few then sat at a table and began to leaf through. We sat quietly not wanting to disturb his concentration. He put the first few books aside and shook his head. 'Nothing,' he said. 'It would help if I had a more precise date.'

'I could ring someone,' said Tash and pulled out her mobile. 'I'll call our friend Dave. He's got it all written down.'

'That would narrow the search,' said the vicar.

Tash went outside to use her phone and the vicar began to tell us about the history of the church, how it had been bombed in the war and parts of it rebuilt and how lucky it was that the records had been unharmed.

'Has the altar always been on the left?' I asked.

The vicar regarded me for a few moments and I felt myself blush. 'An interesting question,' he said finally, 'why do you ask that?'

'For some reason, I thought it was going to be on the right when we walked in. Don't know why.'

'I can tell you exactly why,' said the vicar. 'The altar has always been where it is. That is unchanged but the main entrance to the church used to be on the other side, opposite to the one that we use today. Do you see? Before the original church was bombed, you entered from the other side, then indeed, the altar would have been on the right. If you look carefully when you go back through, you'll see that the original entrance was bricked up.'

'I. . .' I didn't know what to say but Effy's face had lit up.

'Have you seen the original plans of the church somewhere?' he asked me.

'I don't think so,' I said. 'But I must have, mustn't I? Or maybe I noticed the old door had been bricked up without consciously realising.'

'Yeah right,' Effy blurted as Tash came back in and handed the vicar a piece of paper on which she had written down dates that Dave's uncle had given her.

'That makes my task much easier,' said the vicar and he pulled out a large tome from his shelves. After a few minutes flicking through, he stopped at a page and pointed. 'Here we are. Edward Watts, buried in the western part of Highgate Cemetery. I thought so.'

'And what about Henrietta?' asked Tash. 'Henrietta Gleeson.'

'And who was she?' asked the vicar.

'Oh, the governess, I believe,' said Effy. 'Governess to the Watts boys.'

'Do you have her dates?'

I shook my head and made myself remember the image of the woman I'd seen in my regression experience. 'We think she was quite young when she died, maybe in her twenties.'

'OK, let me see. It may take me some time to find her,' said the vicar as he went back to his book and starting flicking through a few pages. A short while later, he looked up. 'And here she is. How sad. You're right, she was a young woman when she died. Twenty-three in fact. She'll be in a different part of the cemetery to the rest of the family because she was a dissenter.'

'What's that?' asked Tash.

'Only Anglicans could be buried on blessed ground in the main part of the cemetery at that time,' the vicar explained. 'Anyone who wasn't Church of England or was an unbeliever or committed suicide, was known as a dissenter and they were buried in unconsecrated ground.'

'Oh my God. Was she a suicide?' I hated to think that.

The vicar shook his head. 'No. That would have been recorded. She would most likely have been an unbeliever or from another religion.'

'Dissenter sounds like an outcast,' I said. I didn't like the idea of anyone being shoved out because of their beliefs.

'That's how it was back then, my dear,' said the vicar and he checked his watch. 'Now I really must go but good luck with your search. You won't be able to go into the cemetery now as it closes at five o'clock in the summertime but go along at the weekend. It's a very interesting place and well worth a look around. Just ask the guide on duty. Most of them know the graves like the back of their hand.'

We trooped back out into the sunlight and Effy was quick to tell Tash all about me knowing the layout of the old church.

Effy turned to me. 'Now that's got to mean something,' she said with a big grin.

'Not really. I could have read about the church somewhere, or seen a documentary about the bombing, that's most likely,' I said, although I wasn't as certain about any of it as I had been.

I hadn't told Effy or Tash about my imaginary childhood friend called Howard. They'd have taken it as more proof that Betty's story was true and it did seem remarkable even though I'd rationalised that there must have been some character on TV that I'd seen as a kid who was called Howard and I'd picked up on it. I kept telling myself that none of it really meant anything, but the coincidences were stacking up. The imaginary friend called Howard, my experience at Fiona's (despite the fact I'd convinced myself that it was a dream), Lily's reading that matched so closely with Betty's – though I'd even tried to rationalise that with the idea that maybe she and Betty had met at a clairvoyants' convention and made up stories together. And now the feeling I'd just had in the church. I knew deep inside that I was running out of arguments against the fact that I might have had past lives. For the first time since I'd been to see Betty, a part of me was beginning to think that there might, just might, be some truth in what she'd said and the proof of it was unfolding in front of me, like clues in a treasure hunt. All I had to do was follow them. But the thought of it being real was seriously creeping me out.

Chapter Sixteen

On Saturday morning, I was up and dressed early. Although I had a ton of work to do for my AS levels, I had to see this Henrietta thing through. I could work in the afternoon – plus, if nothing else, I would get to see Elizabeth Siddal's grave.

Effy and Tash were waiting for me at the top of the lane leading to the cemetery. We were all dressed in light clothes – jeans and T-shirts, mine all black, Tash in pale pinks and Effy in blue jeans but an orange and turquoise top. The skies were clear and it felt odd to be setting off on a tour of a graveyard on such a lovely day. We passed Waterlow Park on our left and then we could see the cemetery beyond. As we got closer, there was a Tudor-style building, with turrets and high wrought iron gates in the middle, leading to a woodland area.

We went to join a small crowd who were waiting for the ten o'clock tour. Some were carrying cameras, others guidebooks.

I glanced across the road where rows of headstones were visible and wondered what the fuss was all about. It looked unremarkable, the same as any cemetery in England, with neat rows of graves.

'There are two parts to the cemetery, the eastern and western,' said Tash. 'The vicar said the Watts grave is in the western part. I went round with my parents a few years ago. It's totally Goth. You'll love it, Jo.'

'I am not a Goth,' I said. Nor did I see why I'd love a tour round a cemetery. It struck me as morbid but I didn't say anything in case they called me a killjoy again.

'I think you should tell the tourists why you're here,' said Effy. 'To gaze upon the grave of your last earthly body. Wuhuhooooo.'

I laughed but it was more through nerves than finding what she'd said funny. Most Saturday mornings I'd do *normal* stuff – catching up on the week, maybe a DIY manicure, check emails, maybe

Facebook, a bit of study – but now here I was in a cemetery going to look for the grave of what could be my former dead body. It doesn't get any weirder, however, there was no going back now. I felt compelled to carry on and see where it led.

At ten on the dot, a man with sandy hair, in his sixties, dressed in an old grey cardigan and corduroy trousers, opened the wrought iron gates and beckoned the group inside.

'Those for the western cemetery this way,' he called. 'Three pounds each. Those here to see Karl Marx's grave, you'll find it opposite in the eastern cemetery.'

'A communist plot,' whispered Effy and Tash giggled.

We dropped our money into a box on the way in and waited with the group in the cobbled courtyard.

Our guide soon motioned for us to follow him and began his talk.

'The building behind is made up of two chapels, one for the Anglicans, one for dissenters. . .'

I looked back at the chapels and then into the woodland where I could see the tops of headstones amidst profuse greenery and trees.

'The western cemetery first opened in 1839 as one of the seven new cemeteries,' the guide continued, 'known as the Magnificent Seven, around the outside of London. The eastern side was added in 1854 and can be toured unaccompanied. About one hundred and seventy thousand persons are buried here in fifty-one thousand graves which vary from the minute plot markers for foundlings and tiny children to the ornate and ostentatious monuments we'll see further on.'

As our group moved on down one of the paths leading away from the courtyard, I looked around. It was nothing like I had imagined. Nature had been left to go completely wild and the crumbling and cracked gravestones were overgrown with moss, weeds and ivy. As we progressed, we saw statues of kneeling angels and bowed Madonnas which were all the more poignant because of their decaying appearance. Despite my nerves, I couldn't help but find the cemetery eerily enchanting, like walking into the perfect Gothic film set. Tash had been right, I did love it.

We walked up a sloping path through a confusion of trees and shrubs. Ivy seemed to have taken over everywhere; untamed it had grown over headstones, up trees, across the winding paths.

'In the early days,' said our guide, 'there were only a handful of trees and row upon row of neatly maintained graves. There was formality and solemnity . . .'

No longer, I thought, *but that's what gives it its charm.*

Effy stopped and read the inscription on one grave. '*Stop stranger there as you go by, as you are now, so once was I,*' she read. '*As I am now, so you shall be, so be prepared to follow me.*'

'To follow you, I'd be content . . . if only I knew which way you went,' I added. That set Tash off laughing and our guide gave her a filthy look.

We read various other gravestones: *to Martha, beloved wife,* or *Bertram, who fell asleep, Emma, who is now in peace.*

'Makes you think, doesn't it? We're all going to die but no one ever talks about it.'

Effy and Tash nodded, serious for a moment.

'Well, we are in a graveyard,' said Tash. 'I wonder where they went. Where *we* go.'

'If anywhere,' I said. 'It would help if, when we got our birth certificates, we got our date of death as well, like a driving licence or credit card, you know, it gives you the date of issue, date of expiry. Then you could prepare.'

'I don't think I'd want to know,' said Effy. 'You might go round being miserable all the time. Like I'm do-oomed.'

'Or maybe you'd make sure you really appreciate each day,' said Tash.

'Oo get us,' said Effy, 'coming over all deep.'

'Hard not to in a place like this,' I said.

The guide frowned at us from the front of the group. 'Shh, over there.'

'I wish we could break away from the group,' I said as I looked at the various pathways through the trees.

'Yeah but I wouldn't want to get lost in here,' said Tash. 'It would be like *The Blair Witch Project* times ten.'

'Times fifty thousand people or however many are buried in here. What if they all came out of their graves at night?' asked Effy.

'We could do the Thriller routine,' I said. We'd done it for an end of term show in Year Seven. I did a few moves and once again the guide at the front frowned at us.

'I read in one of Mum's magazines that they did a survey of the most common last words before dying,' said Tash.

'And what were they?' I asked.

'Oh shit.'

'No. Seriously?' I asked.

Effy nodded and this set us off laughing again. Our tour guide stopped what he was saying. 'Can the group at the back pay attention and have some more respect for where they are, please?'

Tash and I straightened our faces immediately, but poor Effy was off on one of her laughing attacks and had to go into a coughing fit.

'You're having a coffin fit,' whispered Tash.

Of course that made Effy worse and her shoulders were shaking helplessly.

'Be quiet,' I whispered, 'or we'll get thrown out.'

'The Victorians loved the symbolism of death, for example here you have in the angel's hand an upturned torch to symbolise life extinguished,' said the guide as he pointed at a statue that looked like an angel from a Leonardo Da Vinci painting. The guide then pointed at a broken pillar behind him. 'And here's another popular symbol. The pillar is broken, it symbolises life and strength cut off.'

He led us further into the woods and all the time, Effy, Tash and I scanned the headstones looking for the name Watts.

Our guide suddenly stopped at a grave and when I saw the inscription on the headstone, my interest perked up even more. *Elizabeth Siddal.*

'There's a mystery surrounding the Siddal grave,' our guide told us. 'It's said that Rossetti was so consumed with sadness when she died that, as an expression of his grief, he placed a notebook of his poems under her head. Seven years later, his popularity as a poet and artist was diminishing and his agent persuaded him to have the grave opened so that the book could be retrieved. It is said that when the coffin was opened, late one night, Elizabeth's red hair had continued to grow and filled the coffin.'

'Spooky,' I said.

'What a creep,' said Effy. 'Giving her a book of poems then digging her up to get them back. That's so gross.'

'I hope she haunted him,' I said as our guide beckoned us on.

'And now we reach the most famous part of the cemetery,' said the guide. 'Some call it the street or avenue of death or the Egyptian avenue and it leads to the circle of Lebanon.'

As we turned a corner, we came upon a magnificent stone gateway flanked by columns and obelisks worthy of a temple in Egypt. It looked as if it had been built into the side of a hill like the entrance to a cave. As we trooped through the gate, we saw a dark tunnel lined with tall chambers.

'Note the upturned torches on the door frames,' said the guide as he led us through and we looked up at the tall doors towering above us. 'In here are twenty family catacombs.'

'If there are families in here, maybe we'll find the Wattses,' said Effy.

I read the inscriptions next to the doors as we walked through but there were no Wattses. After a while, we came to some steps and climbed up to find another level of graves with an enormous cedar tree in the middle.

'Take a look around,' said the guide, 'and we'll reconvene in a few minutes.'

At last we were free to wander and the three of us split up to cover as much ground as we could. Some of the statues above the graves were works of art and looked like they must have cost a lot of money. I particularly liked the angels. A few minutes later, Effy ran to get me. 'Over here,' she said. 'I've found them!'

I quickly followed her and there, set a short way back from the path, was a marble plinth with a statue of a seated woman in veils. She was leaning against an urn, her head bowed. In her right hand was an upturned torch, in her left, a wreath. I could just about make out the faded writing on the stone:

EDWARD WATTS: 1858—1916 AND HIS
BELOVED WIFE LYDIA: 1860—1933.

Underneath that was:

HOWARD WATTS: 1881—1914
DANIEL WATTS: 1896—1970 AND HIS
BELOVED WIFE ANNIE 1901—1977.

'Daniel must have been the little boy that Henrietta cared for,' said Effy.

'And Howard was only thirty-three when he died. So young,' said Tash.

'Looking at the date, maybe he died in the First World War,' I commented. 'And it looks as if he never married.'

It felt odd to be standing there over a stranger's grave. *What were this family like?* I wondered. Whether I knew them or not, it was eerie to be there. Only a week ago, I was so sure of things. So sure of who I was. Now I felt like I didn't know anything.

'Moving on,' called our guide and beckoned us to go back and join the group. 'I have another group at eleven.'

'Ask him about Henrietta,' urged Tash and Effy raced forward to catch the guide up and we hurried to join her.

'You need to talk to Harry. He looks after the grounds,' the guide told Effy in answer to her question. 'I can't say the name Gleeson is a familiar one, but then some of the graves in the unconsecrated ground are unmarked. Harry will know though, or it will be on a map on the computer. All the graves are listed and accounted for.'

By this time, we were almost back at the courtyard we'd started from. We'd been around in a complete circle and could see a new group waiting at the gates. Our guide said goodbye and went over to greet them.

Effy, Tash and I made our way to the chapel where we found a middle-aged lady at a desk. 'Is Harry here?' I asked.

'You just missed him, love,' she said. 'He'll be back in a couple of hours. Can I help?'

Effy explained about the grave we were looking for.

'No, Harry's your man. I can't help I'm afraid. Come back around two.'

I sighed. I was never going to get any homework done at this rate but no way was I going home now. We'd got so close and found the Watts grave. I had to stay and find Henrietta's.

'OK, let's go and get a strong cappuccino,' I said. 'I need a break from the dead, let's go and live a little.'

Chapter Seventeen

As we passed the florist's shop on the way to the café in Highgate, I glanced in the window. I could see Ben inside. He was holding a bunch of white lilies and standing at the till.

I nudged Effy. 'There's Ben,' I said and she went and virtually pressed her nose up against the window. I prayed that he wouldn't turn around and see us. Effy can be so uncool sometimes. Luckily, he didn't notice us so Effy gave up and we carried on to Costa.

'Flowers, huh,' she said as we went into the café and joined the queue for drinks. 'So he must have a girlfriend somewhere. I wouldn't have taken him for the romantic sort.'

'Speculation,' I said. 'They might be for anyone – his mum or someone's birthday.'

'Maybe they're for you,' said Effy.

'As *if*,' I said. 'I don't think he likes me very much.'

'He invited you to his exhibition,' said Tash. 'He wouldn't have done that if he didn't like you a bit.'

'Whatever,' I said. I didn't care. It was Finn I cared about. I couldn't get him out of my head. His laughing eyes, his cheeky grin. He'd sent me a text that morning: **Need update on fortunetellers. Anything about us yet?** I'd texted back, **Dream on.** He'd texted back a heart. *But does he mean it?* I wondered. I was still confused about whether he was genuinely interested or just a flirt. After the Sunday at the festival, I'd hoped that he might get in touch with me in the week but there had been nothing until the text that morning, not even a poke on Facebook. I'd been tempted to contact him but the thousands of girls on his list of friends on his Facebook page soon stopped me. Maybe it was time to share with Effy and Tash to get their opinion.

We found a table at the back of the café, settled down, and Effy and Tash began to talk about finding the Watts grave.

'How did you feel standing there knowing that you were looking at Howard's grave?' asked Tash.

'Actually I wanted to talk to you both about something else . . . er, OK I'm just going to come out with it. Forget about Howard for a moment and researching some dead guy. I'm interested in a live one.'

Effy sighed. 'Finn,' she said.

'What? What's the problem?' I asked.

'He is. I don't want you to get hurt.'

'Why should I? And at least he's alive! Like . . . here we are looking into this Howard character who you're both convinced is my soulmate and he doesn't even exist any more, but right in front of me is Finn who *does* exist and . . . and he's kind of got to me.'

'He *is* gorgeous,' said Tash, 'but doesn't he have a girlfriend?'

'Yeah. *A girlfriend*,' Effy agreed.

'She wasn't there last week in Highbury. We don't really know anything for sure, do we? Like, how long have they been an item? How serious is it? She could be anyone. A mate even, like I am with Owen. If we're going to research Howard, why can't we research Finn as well?'

Tash nodded. 'Fair point,' she said.

'What about Ben?' asked Effy.

'Ben?' I asked. 'What about him?'

'Do you think it could be a coincidence that we just saw him on the very same day we found Howard's grave?' said Effy.

'A coincidence?' I asked.

Effy nodded. 'Maybe it's a sign,' she said but even she didn't look totally convinced.

'I've barely spoken to Ben and even when I have he's been rude and distant. So no, Effy, I don't think it's a sign that we just saw him in the florist's. Maybe every man we've seen this morning is a contender, a sign. Come on, even you have to admit that to consider Ben just because he was on the high street today is pretty ridiculous.'

Effy pouted and crossed her arms. 'You should keep your options open. Consider other boys, that's all I was saying.'

'I do, I mean, I will. And actually, talking of other boys . . . Has Owen got a girlfriend?'

Effy shook her head. 'Not that I know of and not that he'd tell me if he did. Why?'

'Oh . . . just he was with someone last time I called him. Susie.'

'So you *do* call him?'

'Sometimes.'

'Does it bother you he might be with someone?' asked Tash.

'Course not. I was just interested, that's all. He's my oldest mate, mate that's a boy that is,' I replied, but I noticed Tash shot Effy a look as if to say, yeah right.

'You know it's Finn I like,' I said.

Effy nodded. 'We do. I just don't want you to get your heart broken, that's all.'

'I won't. Look, I'm not stupid. I know that even if Finn isn't seriously attached, he'd still have a queue of girls lining up and I might not have any chance, but he keeps popping up in my mind and he does flirt. He wouldn't do that if he was seriously attached.'

'He might,' said Effy. 'He might be one of these boys who has to prove that he can have anyone. A Casanova. I read an article once which said some boys have something called a Casanova Complex. It's an ego thing, a need to know that they can get off with anyone but behind all the bravado they are actually insecure, hence the need to prove that they can pull over and over again. You don't want to get involved with anyone like that.'

'Insecure and Finn are not two words I'd put together,' I said.

'No,' said Tash, 'and if Jo has got feelings for him, she'd be mad not to at least find out what his situation is.'

'Yes. Thanks, Tash. See, Effy, maybe you've been right all along. Maybe I have been stuck in the past and maybe Betty was right about me being scared to take a risk when it comes to boys. Up till now I've told myself that Finn is out of my league, but I think I have to be brave. Take a chance on love.'

'Sounds good. And if it's meant to be, it will be,' said Tash.

'OK, but if you really do want to go for Finn, sometimes you have to give fate a hand,' said Effy.

'Meaning?' I asked.

'Maybe we should do a ritual,' said Effy. 'Some spell or something to attract the right boy to you.'

I laughed. 'I don't need one of your witchy rituals,' I said. When we were in Year Nine, I had a crush on a boy called Jake. Effy told me to cover a photo of him in sugar, put it under my pillow then sleep on it. It was supposed to make Jake go sweet on me. All it did was get in my hair and make Mum mad because the sheets were so sticky. 'Let's keep it simple – find out where Finn's at and see what happens.'

'You're the boss,' said Effy, 'just tread carefully with him.'

Tash rubbed her hands. 'In the meantime,' she said, 'we could ask around about him.' She sighed and looked out of the window with a dreamy expression in her eyes. 'Actually, you would make a lovely couple. How's the article going by the way?'

'I'm still working on it,' I said. 'There's not been much time with everything else that's been going on.'

'I've been looking at books and CDs about clairvoyants to see if I can get some quotes. Should be good by the time we've finished,' said Effy.

'Maybe you could give the report to Finn in person,' said Tash.

'Maybe I will,' I said as I thought about his text this morning. It was the perfect excuse.

'I could find out his address,' said Effy. 'I told you his parents are looking for a house so Mum will have their details on her files somewhere. I'll look for you next time I'm in.'

Yay. At last, the kind of research I really am interested in! I thought.

After our strong cappuccinos, I felt ready for the next round and we set off once more for the cemetery. Outside the café, the sky had darkened, threatening rain.

'Let's get this thing done before it pours down,' I said to Effy as we marched down Swain's Lane.

By the time we'd got back to the cemetery, there was a thin drizzle of rain and a chill wind beginning to blow. We soon found Harry in the office of one of the chapels. He was a lovely old man with white hair, twinkly blue eyes and a crinkled face. Effy filled him in on who we were looking for.

He listened and nodded. 'I know exactly where she is,' he said. 'I was working up that way only yesterday. Give me a minute and I'll take you there.' He pulled on a raincoat then handed us two umbrellas. 'Here, you might be needing these.'

He led us back into the wood and this time, instead of going to the left, we went to the right.

'It's like a maze,' I said as we followed him along several paths past various headstones. 'How come you don't get lost?'

'It doesn't take long to get to know your way round,' he replied. 'And I've been working here a good long time.'

'Was everyone buried here rich?' asked Tash.

Harry shook his head. 'Not necessarily. They had a different attitude to burial in Victorian times; even the poorest family would save up to make sure their family got a good send-off and a decent site.'

Harry led us away from the main path and over to an overgrown patch of land near the wall by the main road. The graves in this part were very different to the ostentatious and ornate kind we'd seen in the morning. They were humble, small slabs of square stone, some completely covered in moss, others so worn away that there was no inscription left.

Harry led us to an area under a tree and pointed. 'I think this is what you wanted to come and look at,' he said to Effy. 'I remembered the name because I was doing some clearing here just the other day.'

Like the others nearby, it was a small, simple slab of stone but there, just about legible through the moss, was written the name:

HENRIETTA GLEESON, 1882–1905.

My eyes filled with sudden tears which took me by surprise.

'Who was she to you?' asked Harry.

'Oh, just someone I've been told about,' I said. I didn't understand my tears. Until a few weeks ago, the name Henrietta Gleeson meant nothing to me.

'I'll leave you alone for a while,' said Harry. He pointed a short distance away. 'I'll be there when you're ready.'

Effy, Tash and I stood and gazed down at the grave. I could see by their faces that they were as moved as I was. *So there it is,* I thought. *Another grave amongst so many. Henrietta Gleeson. Just another old-fashioned name. Could she really have been me? Could it be true that I am standing here looking down at the grave of someone I used to be, knowing that the spirit that inhabited that body six foot under is no longer down there, because it's in me, looking through my eyes at my own burial site?* I shivered with cold. My thoughts were disturbing. I was beginning to feel like I didn't know what was real any more and who I really was. There was so much I didn't know or understand.

'You OK, Jo?' asked Tash.

I brushed away a tear. 'Yeah, just . . . I guess it's sad that,' I pointed at the headstone, 'it's so simple after the ones we saw this morning and then Harry told us even the poorest family made sure that someone had a good send-off. Henrietta's grave looks so neglected, looks like nobody spent any money on her, whoever she was. Maybe she died poor or alone, forgotten.'

'Until now,' said Effy.

'And so young,' said Tash. 'Only twenty-three.'

I nodded. 'Yeah. Sad.' I felt myself shiver again but wasn't sure if it was the rain or the situation. 'Let's get out of here.'

'I wonder what she was like?' Effy mused as we went over to Harry. 'Who went to her funeral? Was Howard there? How did she die?' An image from my hypnosis session flashed through my mind. The young man bent over the woman in the bed. Could he have been Howard? Could she have been Henrietta? He'd said he'd find her. Could it be possible that she was back as me and Howard was back too, having travelled through time to find her?

As Harry led us back to the courtyard, we were all silent, each of us lost in our thoughts. Seeing Henrietta's grave had given me an idea for a ritual that made sense to me. Not one of Effy's witchy kind. Mine would be a private affair.

Effy suddenly stopped. 'Harry, would you mind if we took another look at a grave we saw this morning? It's near the circle of Lebanon – I wanted to check some dates but couldn't because our tour guide hurried us on. Would you mind?'

'Not at all,' said Harry and he steered us back toward the Egyptian avenue. It didn't take us long to find the grave again and when we got there, we were all taken by surprise. There were fresh flowers on the grave. White lilies. They hadn't been there this morning.

'Someone's tended the grave,' said Tash.

Effy looked around. 'But who?'

'Oh, lots of relatives come and tend the graves,' said Harry. 'Saturday's a popular time and some of the graves are recent, you know—'

'But not that one,' I said.

'No, not that one, but someone comes regularly, every year, to put flowers.'

My mind had gone into a spin. *Who'd left the flowers? Was there a living relative? A grandchild? A son or daughter? Ben? Oh my God! Could it have been him?*

'Ben was buying white lilies this morning,' whispered Effy.

'Is it a sign?' asked Tash.

'No,' I said. 'He could have been buying flowers for anyone.' My brain tried to work out the maths. 'Effy, write down the dates. We need to work out how old any living relative might be.'

'Will do,' said Effy. 'Do you know what this means? He or she might have known Howard or even Henrietta.'

174

'Not possible,' I said. 'But whoever it is could be a son, daughter or grandchild of one of the Watts family.'

'Did this Watts family know your Henrietta then?' asked Harry.

Tash nodded. 'She worked for the family,' she explained.

'She'll be back in three weeks,' said Harry. 'The lady who leaves the flowers.'

So not Ben, I thought. 'A she? You know who it is?' I asked.

Harry nodded. 'I don't have a name but we get to know the regulars by face. I remember her because she comes every year to lay flowers three weeks apart and that's always seemed strange to me.'

'On her own?'

'I've never seen anyone with her.'

'How old?' I asked.

'Not young,' Harry replied. 'She's an elderly lady.'

'Another clue,' I said as we headed back for the gates.

Tash nodded. 'How exciting, and this time we might get answers from the living not the dead!'

Chapter Eighteen

After the cemetery, Tash headed off for the tube leaving Effy and I to make our way back up the village on our own. Effy had a date with Mark, but it wasn't until later so we decided we'd cruise a few shops. On our way to the high street, we passed the Highgate Literary and Scientific Institute.

'Hey, isn't that where the exhibition is?' I said to Effy. 'The one with Ben's photos.'

'Oh yeah. Let's see if it's open,' said Effy. 'See if his photos shed any light on what goes in that head of his, and we could ask him who he was buying flowers for today, if he's there.'

'You can,' I said.

The doors were open and there was a board saying

admission free so we made our way inside the hall. Like Effy, I felt intrigued to see what Ben's pictures would be like.

Inside, partitions had been erected in the centre of the hall making three central corridors, each displaying different exhibitors' photographs. I like looking at exhibitions and neither Effy and I were in a hurry so we slowly went round all the pictures. Some appealed more than others. I liked one girl's portraits taken of the varied colourful characters around Camden Lock. I felt she'd really captured the diversity of people there – Goths, punks, hippies, tourists, the young and the old.

Effy liked a series of landscapes taken with some kind of colour filter over the lens. It made the scenes look surreal, as if they were taken on another planet.

'Here are Ben's,' said Effy when she came to a corner at the back of the hall and saw his name. I went over to join her. *Seasons by Ben Fraser.* His photos were also landscapes but in black and white.

'Hey, these are seriously good,' said Effy.

I looked at the first few. Shots of local scenes around north London. He'd really captured the changing weather of the different seasons. A bright summer's day on Primrose Hill. Kites flying in the sky. A small boy eating an ice cream. A bank of daffo-dils taken on the Heath in spring. A sky exploding with fireworks on Bonfire Night up at Alexandra Palace. A snow scene in winter, sledgers in the fore-ground wrapped up in hats, scarves and gloves.

Effy was looking at a photograph at the far end. 'I know this place,' she said.

I went to join her. The shot was of a landscape, early morning judging by the mist. Everything was white. The location was a playing field with a solitary tree, to the right of which was a pavilion.

'I know where that is,' I said suddenly. 'It's the play-ing field at our old school. The changing rooms were in the pavilion, remember?'

'Oh, yeah, that's right,' she said. 'Freezing in there in the winter.' She moved on to the next picture. I stayed to study the photo. It stirred something in me. As I stared at the image I felt myself transported back, not just to the place or time but to a *feeling*, one of overwhelming sadness. Then it hit me. I used to go there to be alone just after Dad died. There was a spot behind the pavilion which was out of the wind where no-one could see you. It was my secret place. I hadn't allowed myself to cry at home. Mum was so sad, devastated at the loss of Dad, and I didn't want to add to her grief by letting her see my tears although I felt that my world had been torn apart too. I had tried to be brave for her. So much was a blur around that time, so many emotions, so many changes. And then it struck me. Something else about the place. There had been a boy. I'd been there one day and he had appeared out of nowhere. I'd tried to hide my tears in case he asked me what was wrong, but he didn't say anything, just sat on the wooden decking with me like he understood what I was going through. It was a comfort having him there. After that he came a few more times. Not saying anything. Once he took my hand and held it. His hand had felt so warm.

And then time moved on, it was the end of term, the summer holidays. When I went back to school for the new term, I was all cried out. I didn't go back to my secret place and I never saw the boy again. He was older than me so must have gone on to senior school. I never thought about him again and had forgotten all about that time until now. It was too painful, I'd put all the memories from then in a box and locked them away.

I became aware that someone was standing behind me. I turned to see that Ben was watching me.

I turned back to look at the photograph then at Ben and suddenly I realised. 'It was you. You're the boy from the playing field, aren't you?'

He nodded. 'You remember now.'

'I do. I can't believe I forgot. But why? Why did you come and sit with me back then?' I pointed to the photo.

Ben hesitated. 'You looked so alone and . . . and . . .' He shrugged as if he was finding it hard to find the right words. 'It just felt right,' he said finally. He looked vulnerable as he said the words, like he'd let me into his private world for a moment, and in that split second, I could see that behind the cool mask of the sullen boy in shades: he was actually a caring, sensitive person. I wondered if someone had hurt him so much that he felt he had to protect himself and not let anyone too close. I was about to ask why he didn't stay in touch or come back to try to find me after he'd gone on to secondary school when Finn appeared behind him. I felt myself immediately blush. Ben saw the recognition on my face and turned to see who was there. When he turned back, it was as if a curtain had gone down inside of him, his feelings once again hidden from me. As Finn came towards us, I felt myself blush even more and I could see that

Ben noticed. He turned to Finn, nodded hi to him and walked away.

As I watched Ben go, I felt that I should have said more - how great his photos were. How much I'd appreciated him being there so many years ago. But the small crowd in the hall had swallowed him up and Finn was standing next to me looking at Ben's photos. There was no denying the effect Finn had on me - like he radiated some kind of heat that warmed me right down to my toes. I was feeling more and more sure, Finn was The One. Past or present, I didn't care as long as we had some kind of future.

Chapter Nineteen

The following week flew by in a haze of meetings with teachers, reviewing work and projects and discussing objectives for next year, which would be our final one at school. At last, it was Friday and tomorrow was my birthday. I couldn't wait to find out what the girls had planned. They'd been very hush hush about it. All I knew was it was a get-together in the evening, but I wasn't sure if that meant just us or if they'd invited others. They wouldn't say but did let on that the evening had a theme and that they had got my costume sorted. I had mixed feelings about a big celebration if that's what they'd organised. I loved a party as much as the next person, but couldn't help but think about the fact I'd probably be on my own there again.

At least Owen was coming back from uni for the weekend, so I'd have him to talk to. He'd already texted me several times to say how much he was looking forward to seeing me so he must be included in whatever the plans were. I was looking forward to seeing him too. I'd been surprised by my reaction to finding out that he may be with someone and had to question whether I might have feelings for him after all. To let him go, might be to let one of the nicest guys in the world slip through my fingers. Maybe we'd got together too early and I just wasn't ready back then to have met someone as reliable and kind as him. I still felt confused. Was reliable what I wanted now? Not if I was honest. I wanted the feeling I got around Finn. Heat. Bubbles of excitement. *Anticipation.* Finn and I hadn't chatted for long when I'd seen him at Ben's exhibition because he had only dropped in for a short while but there was chemistry there and I was sure he'd felt it too. I could tell by the way he looked into my eyes then down at my mouth and the way he stood close to me with his back turned on everyone else, creating our own private space in the gallery.

As I gathered up my things to leave school, I texted Effy and Tash to let them know I was going home and that I'd see them the next day. They still had work to do in the art room so it was the perfect time to put into practice the ritual idea that I'd had the week before. It was something I wanted to do alone.

I caught the bus home and found a few of Mum's small gardening tools which I put in my bag. Next I went up to the florist's in the village where I bought a bunch of white rosebuds before making my way to the cemetery. Luckily Harry was at the front lodge and when I told him what I wanted to do, he let me through and escorted me to Henrietta's grave.

'Just give me a shout if you need anything,' he said as he started back to the lodge. 'I have lots of tools you can borrow.'

When he'd gone, I set about tidying up the grave. I pulled up the weeds, scrubbed the moss off the stone and dug over the earth. I decided to leave the trail of ivy that had grown up the headstone – the green looked pretty against the pale stone. I placed the roses I'd bought at the top of the grave and stood up. It looked much better, not so sad and neglected. Looking after Henrietta's grave felt therapeutic, like clearing away cobwebs of the past. Mine and hers. Effy would be proud of me, although knowing her, she'd probably have wanted to light a joss stick and do an Native American dance as well.

I checked to see that no-one was around. All was silent. 'There you go, Henrietta, whoever you were,' I said to the headstone. 'I don't know exactly what you went through, but if it's true, and you were me once, I want to tell you that you and me, we're moving on. I'm going to embrace life and take a few chances – especially on love.'

As I stood there in the dappled light, I felt a sensation of peace come over me. I felt Henrietta approved. Or I approved. How *I* related to Henrietta was so mixed up in my head.

My phone rang, shattering the quiet of the cemetery. I almost jumped out of my skin.

It was Effy. 'Hey you, where are you?'

'Oh . . . hi. Just on my way home. You?'

'I just got to my mum's agency. You'll never guess what. Finn was in with his family when I got here. Talking through some possible houses.'

'Really?'

'Well, he was with the girl, you know, the one from the Heath and the café.'

My spirits sank. So much for my ritual about moving on, taking a chance on love. Effy was calling to tell me that it *was* serious with the girl. It must be if she was involved in the house-hunting.

'She's his sister, Jo. His *sister*!'

'Sister? You're kidding?'

'No. Her name's Darcy. She's really nice. And there's more. I got her on her own and asked, really casually, if Finn was involved with anyone.'

I knew Effy and casual. Not something she did at all well. 'You didn't say I was into him, did you?'

'No. Course not. No, I was really good. I said Finn must have loads of girls after him seeing as he's in the band and that. And she said, he does. I said, is he with anyone at the moment? She said, not that she knew about and that Finn tells her everything, although he had mentioned – and this is the best part – that he had met someone recently that he thought might be special. It could be you, Jo!'

My spirits began to soar. 'That's fantastic. Thanks, Effy.'

'You're welcome. And there's even more . . . oh. Can't tell you. Um. You'll find out tomorrow. Listen, got to go. Loads to organise for tomorrow night. Be at mine at six o'clock, OK?'

'OK. I'll be there.'

After the call, I gathered up my things and headed back for the lodge. The timing of my moving-on ritual had been perfect, as had Effy's call. It felt like the universe was responding. Finn was free. But what had Effy meant by 'there's more'? Was Finn somehow involved in my birthday surprise? Were her and Tash going to have him gift-wrapped and delivered by parcel express? Now that idea did appeal. Suddenly the weekend was looking a lot brighter and as I walked back to the lodge, my whole world felt lighter.

When I got to the road, it occurred to me that if Finn had been at the estate agent's, he might still be in the village. I raced up the lane, then slowed down, so that if I did accidentally-on-purpose bump into him, I didn't look like a beetroot.

I strolled down the high street, acting like I was window-shopping but actually looking to see if Finn was in any of the shops. I passed the estate agency. I could see Mrs Davis at her desk but there was no sign of Finn or Effy. I passed Costa. I even went in and bought a cereal bar but still no Finn. He wasn't in our regular café either.

This is mad, I told myself after I'd looked in the window at Café Rouge. *It's one thing being more positive about the future but another trooping about like a sad loser.* I set off for the bus stop. *Tomorrow, maybe I'll see Finn tomorrow.*

'Hey, you, stop stalking me,' said a male voice.

I turned around to see Finn standing behind me. I went bright red. Had he seen me looking in all the shops? How long had he been behind me? *Oh shut up, Jo,* I told myself. *He couldn't know that Effy had told me he was in Highgate. He couldn't know I was looking for him. He can't see in my head.* All the same, I felt like I'd been caught out.

'Er . . . Hi. Ha ha, me stalking you? Er, maybe you hadn't noticed that you're behind me. I think that when stalking, it's common for the stalker to be behind,' I said and realised that I was blabbering.

'I like to be different,' said Finn.

He's teasing me, I thought, *isn't he? Yes. He is. God, I must relax, not be so intense.*

'So. *Are* you following me?' I asked.

He laughed. 'Ah and there was me trying to be discreet. I'll never get my stalker's badge, will I? Nah. I just saw you across the street. So what you been up to?'

'You'd never believe me if I told you.'

'You said that last time.'

188

'Did I? Oh. Yes, well, I like to be consistent. So what have *you* been up to?'

'With Mum and Dad looking at houses,' he said, 'and also, checking out wedding venues. My eldest sister's getting married in the autumn.'

'How many sisters have you got?'

'Two. Darcy and Michelle. Michelle's the one getting married.'

'Will you be pageboy?'

'Think I'd look cute in a wee velvet suit? Nah. She wants my band to do the music, that will be my contribution.'

'Where's she getting married?'

'St George's,' Finn replied. 'Church at the back of the square. Do you know it?'

'I do. Least now I do.' A thought flashed into my mind. Wedding? St George's. 'Have you been inside?'

'Yeah. We all went a few weeks ago to check it out.'

'Did the church seem familiar?'

Finn gave me a strange look. 'Familiar how?'

'Oh . . . don't know, that is, when I went in, I felt the altar was in the wrong place.'

Finn looked baffled. 'You going into interior design?'

'No.'

'Architecture?'

'No. I—'

A black BMW honked a short distance away. 'Finn,' called the driver. I looked over. An older man was at the driving wheel, Finn's dad by the look of him.

'Sorry, I've got to go,' he said. 'See you tomorrow.'

'Tomorrow?'

I could tell by Finn's face that he'd realised that he wasn't supposed to let on that he knew about my birthday. 'I mean around. Tomorrow, next day, soon.'

I laughed. He was definitely in on whatever surprise Effy and Tash had organised. 'Yeah.'

He turned to go then glanced back. 'Oh, I meant to ask you, how's the article coming along?'

'Slowly,' I said.

He gave me a wide grin and looked me up and down in a suggestive way. 'That's how I like it.'

If I was red before, I was purple now. Someone let out a strange high-pitched giggle. Oh Lord! It was me. I turned away before I did or said anything else stupid.

Finn got into the waiting car which then roared off. There was no denying it. Major flirting had just taken place. As I reached my bus stop, I realised that I was grinning like an idiot.

Chapter Twenty

When I got to Effy's the next day, she showed me the invite that she and Tash had sent out.

> Come As You Were
> A reincarnation party at
> 228 Trinder Road, north London N6
> Saturday June 2nd, 7.30 onwards
> Dress up as whoever you think you might
> have been in a past life.

'Brilliant idea for a party but I have nothing to wear,' I said as I sat on Effy's bed. 'I didn't come prepared.'

'Sorted,' said Tash and she produced an Edwardian dress from Effy's wardrobe. 'We got it from the fancy dress hire shop when we got our costumes. Put your hair up and you'll look the part perfectly.'

I didn't have to ask what part. It had been decided for me. Henrietta.

The dress was fabulous, deep plum-coloured velvet with a high buttoned neck and nipped-in waist. It fitted perfectly and when I did my hair, I looked every bit the governess.

'I look like Mary Poppins,' I said as I took in my reflection.

'Supercalifragilistic. Really suits you,' said Effy as she added big gold earrings to her outfit. She was going as an Egyptian dancer and Tash as Guinevere in a simple white dress with a crown of flowers on top of her loose hair which for once she'd let curl.

A squirt of my Guerlain Jicky perfume (my birthday present from Mum – she knew it was my favourite) and we were ready. We made our way down to the basement where the party was to be held. Effy's mum and dad were still in the house but had retired to the top floor for the evening. The lower floor has always been Owen and Effy's. It changed from a nursery to a den as they grew up. It's a lovely space that opens out through French windows into the garden at the back, it has a bathroom and loo and what used to be an au pair's room is now Owen's bedroom and study at the front. This evening, the back doors were open onto a lovely summer evening and Dave, dressed as Sir Lancelot, was ready to meet guests with a tray of fruit punch out on the terrace area. Owen, dressed as an ancient Greek in a toga and sandals, was out there with him. He was busy filling bowls with crisps and tortilla chips.

'Hmm, nice legs,' I said.

He turned and looked me up and down. 'Thanks and wow, you look amazing. Seriously.' He put down his bag of supplies, gave me a hug and pulled me over to a quiet corner. 'So how have you been?'

'Good,' I said but I took a step back from him. I didn't want Finn to arrive, see me in a close tête à tête, then get the wrong idea.

Owen noticed that I was keeping my distance and, for a second, a flash of hurt crossed his face. 'I . . . I wondered if we could get some time alone? Doesn't have to be tonight as you'll be busy chatting to everyone at the party.'

I glanced at the door where people were beginning to arrive. 'Course,' I said. 'Maybe in the summer when you're back for longer. We'll have weeks to hang out with the gang then.'

Owen looked directly into my eyes. 'I meant just us. We don't always have to hang out with the others.'

'That's true. Talking of which, who's this Susie then?'

Owen shrugged a shoulder. 'Just a mate. No-one special. Listen, Jo, I . . . I want to talk to you.' My heart went out to him. This was Owen. One of my oldest friends and I did have feelings for him, tender feelings. I wouldn't hurt him for the world.

'Sure. Course,' I said. 'We'll do something soon. Just us.'

Luckily I was saved by Mark's arrival. He was dressed as an Egyptian king and was followed soon after by the Pope, Rasputin and the Queen of Sheba. Someone dressed as a pig came in from the garden and headed straight for the table of food making *oink oink* sounds that cracked us all up. It was a good spread. My mum had paid for some of it and Effy had asked people to bring contributions, then Tash, Owen, Mark and Dave had put it all together. Quiches, French bread, cheeses, coleslaw, hummus, taramasalata, lots of crisps and dips were all laid out with paper plates to the side.

The pig wasn't the only strange costume; Ben Fraser arrived wearing black bin liners and his usual shades. I felt a rush of anticipation on seeing him. If Ben was here, Finn couldn't be far behind.

'What are you supposed to be?' asked Tash.

'A black hole,' he replied. 'What else?'

'Obvi,' said Effy.

I cracked up and even Ben laughed. 'Each to his own,' I said. 'I guess everyone will interpret the theme their own way, depending on what they believe.'

'Or depending on what costume suits them,' said Tash. 'I don't really believe I was Guinevere. I just like the look.'

Ben turned back to me and thrust a card into my hand. 'You look good.'

'Thanks,' I said.

Tash whipped the card away from me. 'I'll take that,' she said and went and put it on a small pile on a table in the corner.

'Sorry about my bossy friend,' I said to Ben. 'Her and Effy do like to organise.'

Ben looked around. 'It's nice. Nice to have mates who are there for you.'

'Are you good mates with everyone in the band?' I asked. 'Or is it just a business arrangement?' I was hoping to get him talking about Finn.

'Bit of both,' said Ben. 'We have to get on because we spend so much time together.'

'Food,' Dave called from the buffet table. He came

towards us with a couple of plates laden with pizza. He gave one plate to Ben. 'Give us a hand, will you, and hand out some of this while it's hot.'

'Sure,' said Ben.

'I told you my friends were bossy,' I said.

'It's cool. It's your birthday. You should be princess for the day,' he said, smiled then went off with Dave. I was beginning to warm to Ben. My silent companion from my sad days in junior school and he clearly had a good sense of humour judging by his mad bin liner costume. Maybe he would be worth getting to know better.

After he'd gone, Owen moved back over to me with a worried look on his face. 'Who's he?'

'No-one really,' I was able to say truthfully. 'Just a guy from Minted, the bass player in fact.'

I could see he was relieved. 'Oh yeah. I thought he looked familiar,' he said.

The rooms and garden soon began to fill up with various kings, queens, a nun, a vicar, Marilyn Monroe, Jimi Hendrix and a few animals. It appeared that Effy had invited half of our year plus some people we knew from the year above. Dave and Mark had invited some boys from their school too. Luckily everyone arrived laden with food and drinks for the table. I watched a headless Mary Queen of Scots head for the buffet. She'd fastened her dress over her hair and was carrying a papier mâché head under her arm. *Very inventive but perhaps not the wisest costume*, I thought as she walked into a wall.

'I see Mary's out of her head again,' Effy quipped as she sashayed past.

'You've invited loads of people,' I said. 'Sure your mum and dad are OK with it?'

Effy nodded. 'You know they love a full house.' I did. Effy and Owen's parents were very social and there were always people over, whether for a big Sunday lunch or spontaneous drinks party.

'Um, so seeing as Ben is here . . . any chance you invited Finn?' I asked. I tried to act like I didn't know.

Tash grinned. 'Course we invited Finn.'

'A birthday surprise,' said Effy. 'Though I do think Owen is keener than ever.' My face must have given away my reaction to that news and Effy put her hand on my arm. 'But hey, even though he's my brother, if it's not true love, I'm certainly not going to push it.'

'There are different kinds of love,' I said. 'True love, safe love, crazy love, love for chocolate, love for friends. A hundred varieties of love and how I feel about Owen is in there somewhere.'

Already the atmosphere was bubbling as people greeted each other and saw who'd dressed up as who. I wondered who Finn would come as. Casanova? Some romantic hero, I was sure of that. *It will be so cool if Finn comes as an Edwardian gentleman*, I thought, *then we'll be the perfect match.*

Tracey O'Neill and Chantelle Robinson made their entrance next. Tracey had come as Peter Pan, a fictional character so not possibly someone she might have been in a past life but it didn't matter, especially not to the boys, most of whom did double takes when she walked past. Her amazing, curvy body, tiny waist and great legs were shown off to great effect by the short tunic she was wearing with a wide leather belt slung round her hips. She's very pretty with cropped auburn hair and as I watched the boys ogling her and Chantelle, who was wearing nothing but a bath towel, I wondered if I should have insisted on wearing a sexier outfit. I liked the dress the girls had found me but with its high neck, I was beginning to feel a tad prim and proper in it.

'Who are you supposed to be?' Tash asked Chantelle.

'The invite said come as you were. I was in the bath about half an hour ago,' she replied, 'so I've come as I was.'

'Brilliant,' said Tash.

Tracey pulled a bottle out of her bag and offered it to me. Vodka.

'Oh, no thanks,' I said.

She shrugged then laughed. 'Staying in character, are you?'

Now I really did feel prim and proper.

Effy was busy Egyptian dancing with Mark so I went through to the garden to see who was out there. Behind me, there was a sudden round of applause. I looked to see what was happening and saw a group of people gathered at the door. I went back inside and jostled my way through the crowd to see that the commotion had been caused by Finn's grand entrance. He wasn't dressed as my romantic hero, instead he'd come as a ballet dancer in a pink tutu and a diamanté tiara on his head. His costume didn't cover his hairy legs and sneakers though. He was prancing around doing the dance of the dying swan. Curiously, even though dressed as a girl, he looked more attractive than ever.

He noticed me, grinned and pirouetted over. 'What do you think?' he asked.

'Very . . . pretty,' I said as Elvis Presley handed him a drink.

I looked down at his Converse Allstars. 'Didn't they do ballet shoes in size ten?'

'Afraid not. Hey, you look good. I always fancied Mary Poppins.'

'I'm *not* Mary Poppins,' I said as Owen passed by. He heard what Finn had said and glanced at me. In an instant, I knew he could see that I was attracted to Finn. He'd known me all my life. He attempted a grin but I could see it was a cover-up. He spun around and headed back inside almost knocking Effy over on his way.

She came over to join us. 'Congratulations, Finn,' she said. 'You're the first person to come in a different gender to the one in this life.'

Finn looked mystified. 'Meaning?'

'Apparently souls don't always stay the same sex on their journey through time. We have some lives as women, some as men. You may well have been a woman in a past life.'

Finn looked at me, then back at Effy, then put his arm around her. 'Jo, your mate doesn't half talk some shite.'

With that he wandered off towards the drinks table where he'd seen Ben. I also noticed Tracey appeared to be adding the vodka to the punch. *Like a moth to a flame*, I thought as I saw her clock Finn then go into full flirt mode and, the cheek of him, he even glanced over at me to see if I was watching. I stuck my tongue out at him but it was Ben who saw it and nudged Finn. For a moment, I thought Finn was going to come back over to me, but then Effy and Tash appeared with a big cake with candles and everyone sang a rousing chorus of 'Happy Birthday'.

'Make a wish,' said Effy when they'd finished.

I took a quick look around the room at all my mates looking at me with affection: Owen, Dave, Mark, people from school and Finn's smiling face there amongst them. It didn't get any better. *I wish that Finn is The One*, I thought as I blew out the candles.

Everyone cheered, then a great fuss was made of cutting the cake and making sure everyone got a piece. I looked around to find Finn to give him an extra-large piece but he seemed to have disappeared. I realised I couldn't see Tracey either. *Doesn't mean they're together*, I told myself. *Doesn't mean they're together*.

I chatted to various people but was finding it hard to focus. I had a nagging feeling in the pit of my stomach. I made my way into the hall where there was a queue for the bathroom. It was occupied.

Dave banged on the door. 'Come on, there are people bursting out here.'

I heard a stifled giggle as the door was unlocked. Out came a dishevelled Finn, his tiara in his hand and his lippie smeared up his cheek. He wasn't alone. Tracey was with him, leaning into him with one arm slung around his neck.

I turned away and came face to face with Owen. He saw what was happening straight away and that I was upset. He looked over at Finn, then back to me, and the expression on his face mirrored mine.

As if things couldn't get more awkward, Ben appeared behind Owen. He also registered what was going on and looked at me to see my reaction. And then Finn noticed me standing there. With Tracey still draped around him, he shrugged his shoulders and gave me a helpless look as if to say, what can I do?

I looked from Owen to Ben to Finn. They all seemed to be looking at me as though they felt sorry for me. *I guess the whole world knows that I'm just another sad loser with a crush on Finn O'Brady, I* thought as I pushed past them. *Why oh why does love have to be so complicated and the one boy I truly want is with another girl?* I asked myself as I made a dash for the garden where I burst into tears. *Happy Birthday to me. Not.*

Chapter Twenty-one

I woke the next morning with a throbbing head. It felt unfair as I hadn't even had any of the spiked punch last night. I heaved myself out of bed and caught a glimpse of myself in the mirror opposite. Peering back at me was a blotchy face with dark circles under bloodshot eyes. 'Perfect English rose,' I told my reflection. 'Wilting and eaten by greenfly.'

I cast my mind back to the party. After I'd seen Finn and Tracey, Effy and Tash had rallied round and done their best to cheer me up. I tried to put a brave face on, like, oh I don't care, but they saw through it and I felt a killjoy after all the effort they'd put in.

'He would have done your head in anyway,' Effy'd said as we cleared up the debris after people had gone.

'You have to let love go,' Tash had said as she gave me a big hug. 'Let it go and if it comes back to you, great. If not, it wasn't meant to be.'

'Not meant to be then,' I'd said as I dumped a pile of paper plates in a bin.

Finn and Tracey had disappeared soon after the bathroom incident, taking with them any feeling of excitement I'd felt earlier at the party. Owen had made himself scarce too and I felt his absence just as strongly. He was one of my best friends and I'd hurt him as much as Finn had hurt me. Ben must have disappeared too because I don't remember seeing him later either.

Love sucks, I thought as I splashed my face with water. Maybe my outfit had been the problem. I should have worn something more revealing, more seductive, gone as a femme fatale like some of the other girls, and then maybe Finn wouldn't have gone off with someone else. Edwardian governess? Hardly hot. What boy wants to snog Mary Poppins when there's a scantily clad five-star babe like Tracey in the vicinity?

As I got dressed, I tried to tell myself that Finn wasn't mine anyway. We weren't in a relationship, so what was my problem? I felt wretched about Owen too. I wished I could feel for him what I felt for Finn. What was wrong with me? Owen was a boy I liked and who liked me so why was I so hung up on another boy who clearly wasn't into me and appeared to collect girls like other boys collected CDs?

Because Finn'd flirted with me, that's why. And when he did, I'd felt alive, like we could have had something special. *Argh. I have been an idiot. I am so over you, Finn O'Brady, I told myself. End of. Amen. Fini.*

Maybe it's true, my mind nattered on. *Just as Betty said. I have the belief that love is unrequited on my brain, and like poor old Henrietta, I will always be alone.*

'No.' I told my reflection. 'I am not Henrietta. I am me. Jo. And I will find love. I will. Someone who doesn't mess with my head. I am not going to give in to loser mode.' For the briefest second, I had the weirdest sensation. I was looking in the mirror but someone else was looking back at me. A girl with dark hair like me, but a different face. It was the girl I'd seen in my hypnosis session lying on the bed.

I bent over and splashed my face with cold water and looked in the mirror again. She'd gone. *I'm just tired,* I told myself. *Imagining things after an overemotional night.* 'I am not Henrietta,' I said out loud.

A knock at my door made me almost jump out of my skin. Mum opened the door. 'Who are you talking to?' she asked.

'No-one. Er . . . myself.'

Mum shrugged. 'You haven't opened your pile of cards from last night,' she said, handing me a small stash of envelopes.

Had Finn left one? I wondered as I ripped the envelopes open. Maybe written an apology. How would I feel about that? Would it make everything all right?

Mum went down to make us some tea while I ripped open the cards. Lots of lovely birthday greetings from friends. I came to the last card. Would this be the one from Finn?

The card was a black and white shot of children playing with balloons on the Heath, their laughing faces upturned to the sky. A happy photograph taken on a summer's day. I looked at the back. As I'd thought, it was one of Ben Fraser's. I looked inside.

Wishing you a happy birthday.
Maybe we could meet up some time? *Ben* 07776868000

Sweet, I thought but I couldn't really appreciate it. I was too disappointed that there was nothing from Finn.

My mobile bleeped that I had a message and then another one. I pulled my phone out and glanced at the screen. The first was from Owen.

I will always be there for you, Owen X

Owen, I thought as I remembered that he'd said he wanted to talk. *What am I going to do about you? I can't bear the thought that I might hurt you more than I have already.*

My heart skipped a beat when I saw that the second text was from Finn.

It wasn't what it seemed. Call me. Finn.

Yeah sure, I thought as I switched the phone off and sat on my bed. *You might cause a major meltdown inside of me, Finn O'Brady, but are you worth it?*

Five minutes later, I turned my phone on and read the message again. Despite my earlier resolutions, I was intrigued to know what lame excuse he was going to come out with. *Should I text back or call?* I wondered. *Or should I leave it a day or two, or a week even, to show I really am cool and don't care. I could call then and say, oh yeah, you texted? Sorry. Been busy . . . But can I wait that long? I want to know now what he has to say.* Effy's words from the night before came back to me. 'He'll do your head in,' she'd said. *Already happening*, I thought. *Argh. What to do? Be strong. No boy wants an emotional wreck. I know what I'll do. I'll show you just how unaffected I am by you, Finn O'Brady.*

I picked up Ben's card, went back to my phone and called his number before I could change my mind.

Chapter Twenty-two

I'd arranged to see Ben in Costa in Highgate village. He was already there when I arrived, seated at a bar stool at the window overlooking the street.

'You recovered from the party?' he asked as I took the stool next to him.

'Oh yes,' I said. '*Well* recovered.' I meant from Finn not just the party. 'You left early?'

Ben shrugged but didn't elaborate. I wondered if I'd imagined his face when he saw how upset I was over Finn, but he wasn't giving anything away. He asked what I'd like from the counter and went off to get me a drink.

'I liked your photos,' I said when he came back with two steaming mugs of hot chocolate and a huge slice of carrot cake with lemon icing and two forks. 'The ones in the exhibition.'

'Thanks.' He half smiled. 'You like carrot cake?'

'My favourite actually.' I wasn't lying.

Ben handed me a fork. 'Mine too. Tuck in.'

'And . . . about you sitting with me all those years ago. Back in junior school. I never got to thank you.'

Ben shrugged again. 'No need. Anyway, long time ago, hey?'

'It was just after my dad died. We never spoke so you must have wondered what it was all about.'

'I figured something like that. I seem to remember hearing about it. You know how news travels at school.'

'I liked that you didn't say much. Everyone was telling me that I should eat. I should talk. I should feel this or that. You didn't. You were just with me, you let me be and that's what I needed. I know it's a few years late but thank you.'

'You're welcome.'

We both stared out of the window for a while as if we were wondering what to say next.

'About the article . . .' we said at the same time, then laughed.

'You start,' said Ben.

'OK. So. Yes. You asked what angle I was going to take. I thought I'd just write up the clairvoyants Effy and I visited without giving my opinion, just state the facts and let the reader decide.'

'And the facts are?'

I laughed. 'Hah. Bit of a muddle really. Some of them went on about past lives I'd supposedly had. I'm not sure where I stand on that. What do you think?'

'I think we live, we die. All we can be sure about is that we're alive now.'

'So you don't believe in reincarnation then?'

'I don't,' he said, then he smiled. I liked him when he smiled, like he lit up from inside. 'Imagine what chaos it would be if we all remembered our past lives.'

'Meaning?'

'Oh, like . . . say someone who'd done something in a past life, like a writer or artist, who'd died in poverty then later their work became really successful, what if they remembered who they were and wanted to cash in on it?'

'Like who?'

'Umm . . . like Jane Austen. She had moderate success when she was alive but who hasn't heard of her now? Her books must have sold millions since she died, not to mention the film and TV adaptations. What if she was back in this life, remembered that she was Jane and wanted her royalties?'

I laughed. 'Yes. Wow. I see what you mean. Publishers would freak but then, how would you prove it to them?'

'Exactly. It's an interesting notion,' Ben continued.

'So who else?' I asked. 'Imagine who else might be back and who as?'

'Your turn' said Ben.

'OK, give me a name.'

'St Francis of Assissi.'

'Obvi,' I replied. 'A vet.'

Ben laughed out loud. 'Lancelot and Guinevere?'

'They'd run a dating agency.'

Ben laughed again and as we drank our drinks and chatted away, I realised there was more to him than the 'scowler'.

'What about God? Do you believe in God?' I asked.

'Wow. Heavy stuff for a Sunday morning.'

'It's *because* it's Sunday,' I said. 'Do you believe in God?'

'I have a theory about God,' said Ben. 'I think there are three gods. Brothers, in fact. God the good – he made the flowers and the sunsets and all that kind of stuff. God the bad. He's nasty and is the one who made wasps. I mean what's the point of them?'

'And sharks,' I said.

'Yeah and sharks,' agreed Ben.

'What about the third one?'

'God the stupid,' said Ben. 'Not as bright as the other two. Everything he made is flawed, hence all the cock-ups on the planet.'

This time it was my turn to laugh out loud. 'Good theory,' I said. 'I like that.' I was beginning to like Ben now that I was getting to know the real him. He was funny and quirky. It was like I was seeing him properly for the first time. He had kind, intelligent eyes, eyes that were looking into mine, searching. For a moment, we connected and I felt a sweet lurch deep inside of me. It felt so intense and unexpected that I had to look away.

I picked up my fork and cut a small piece of carrot cake. 'Um . . . Do you have a girlfriend, Ben?'

He raised an eyebrow. 'Direct, aren't you?'

'Just I saw you one day buying flowers,' I said and pointed out the window towards the florist's.

'That must have been for my mum's birthday,' he said. 'Have you been checking up on me?'

'No, just asking.'

'Well, no, I don't have a girlfriend. What about you?' Ben asked.

'Do I have a girlfriend?' I teased.

'No. Boyfriend . . . I got the impression you like Finn.'

'No way. He'd do my head in.'

'Yours and plenty others.'

'Exactly,' I said. 'I like being single anyway. Love does your head in.'

Ben nodded. 'Exactly my sentiments.'

'One of the clairvoyants said I have it imprinted on my subconscious mind that love is painful.'

A look of sadness flashed across Ben's face. 'It can be if the person you like doesn't feel the same or doesn't even notice you.'

I studied his face. I wasn't sure if he was talking about me and Finn or about himself. 'Or someone you love dies,' I said. 'I think the clairvoyant might have been right but it wasn't as . . . er . . . complicated as she was making out. Simple truth is that I lost someone close when I was very young. That sort of thing is bound to affect you, isn't it?' I was surprised I was talking to Ben like this. Saying things that were really private. He reached over, took my hand and

215

squeezed it like he understood. *Time to change the subject*, I decided. It suddenly felt too intimate. 'So what about your photos for the article then?'

'I'm going to take a whole range,' he replied, letting go of my hand. 'Finn will probably only use one or two but I might do a whole load. I like the theme.'

At the mention of Finn again, I felt my stomach turn over. I wished I could never see him again but there was no chance of that while we were on the *Chillaxin* team together. *I am not going to think about you, Finn O'Brady*, I told myself. I glanced over at Ben. He knew Finn well. Maybe he'd have some advice.

'Ben?'

'Yeah?'

'What would you do if you met someone and . . . it wasn't exactly working out or, that is, you don't know what's going on.'

'Who?'

'Oh, just someone I've met recently. I like him but don't know how to tell him in case he doesn't feel the same way.'

Ben studied me. 'Someone you've met *recently*, you say?'

I nodded. 'I feel like I've had enough of all the negative stuff about how love can do your head in and being afraid to let something happen. Sometimes you have to take a chance, yeah?'

Ben thought for a few moments and I swear he blushed. Just slightly. 'Yes. I think you do. You should tell him how you feel. You might find out he's been feeling the same way. Boys fear rejection just as much as girls, you know.'

Our eyes locked together again but we were interrupted by the sound of my mobile. I pulled it out and glanced at the screen. It was Effy.

'Go ahead,' said Ben indicating that I should take the call.

'Where are you?' Effy asked as soon as I picked up.

'Highgate.' I motioned to Ben that I was going to take the call outside. He nodded.

'Are you alone?' she asked.

'Yes,' I said once I'd got outside.

'I need to talk to you about Finn.'

'I'm so over him, Effy. And you don't need to worry.' I glanced back at Ben inside the café. I'd felt something in there. Unexpected but undeniable. 'I'm not pining or wallowing in misery over that loser.'

'No. We got it wrong. It wasn't what it seemed last night.'

'What do you mean?'

'I found out what happened. Apparently Tracey had drunk a bucketload before she came to the party. She was well out of her head by the time she got to us. Finn was in the loo when she banged on the door to be let in and when he opened the door, she rushed in and puked her guts out. Then she tried to snog him.'

'*Ew*.'

'I know. Ew. Anyway, after that, he took her home. So actually, even though I hate to admit it, he was the hero last night.'

I didn't know what to say; how could I have got it so wrong.

'Jo? Jo, are you there?' Effy's voice interrupted my thoughts.

'Yes, I . . . Oh hell.'

'Why oh hell? Isn't this a good thing?'

'Yes, it is, it's just . . . I'm in Highgate with Ben.'

'Ben, bass player Ben?'

'Yes.'

'What are you doing with him?'

'I . . .' I glanced back inside. 'Nothing. I . . . I don't know.' I *didn't* know. I was beginning to like Ben. He was fun and had interesting ideas. I liked that too and I'd felt a connection back in the café. I was sure he'd felt it too. But then I'd been sure that there'd been a connection with Finn as well. I'd got it wrong about him and Tracey. Maybe there was a chance for us after all. I glanced back at the café. Ben was watching me, then turned away.

'Listen, Effy, I've got to go. I'll call you later, OK?' I hung up the phone before Effy could launch her inquisition about why I was out with Ben. I went back into the café. 'I'm going to take a chance, Ben. I'm going to tell the boy how I feel,' I said as I sat next to him.

Ben took a sharp intake of breath, looked away then back at me. '. . . OK.'

'Thanks for your advice,' I continued. 'It really helped. I'm going to call him when I get home.'

'Call *him*?'

'Yes. I suppose you might as well know. It's Finn. I know he has loads of girls interested in him, but I have to take a chance.'

Ben's face changed suddenly. The open expression he'd had earlier closed shut. 'Of course,' he said as he turned away slightly and shook his head. 'Finn.'

As I left the café, I felt more mixed up than ever. Finn wasn't with Tracey after all. *That's good, isn't it?* I asked myself. *So why do I feel weird?* I should have felt happier about it but something deep inside of me felt regret, like I'd said or done the wrong thing. Was it because I'd felt something starting to happen with Ben? I turned back to see if he was watching me go. His seat was empty.

Chapter Twenty-three

By the time my next hypnotherapy appointment came round the week after my party, I felt that I needed a session purely to relax. I hadn't been sleeping again, not because of the recurring dream I'd had previously, but because I'd started having a new dream. I was on a game show and had to decide between three boys: Owen, Ben or Finn. It was driving me mad. Owen had gone back to university but had sent me an email saying that he'd like to get together next time he was back. I'd emailed Finn to say I was sorry I hadn't got to spend more time with him at the party and he'd replied saying we should get together soon. And Ben . . . He kept popping up in my thoughts. There was something about him that had got to me.

'And what about past lives, Jo? Have you given that any more thought?' asked Fiona as I settled onto the couch.

'Sort of but honestly, I don't know what to think. I've been feeling a bit crazy lately, like I don't know who I am any more or what's real. Plus I've had too much drama going on in *this* life to have any time to worry about past lives.'

'Don't stress over it,' said Fiona. 'There are times in life when you have to step back and let things unfold and not try and force the issue. So, are you ready? I think we made some real progress in our last session, so let's see if we can go any further this time.'

I nodded and closed my eyes. *I'm going to be asleep in seconds*, I thought. The atmosphere was so peaceful in Fiona's office and the scent of lavender and frankincense that she burnt added to the calm.

'Do you mind if I record the session again, Jo?'

'Sure, go ahead,' I said, though I had the feeling that the only sound I was going to make today was zzzzz.

Fiona began to talk softly. 'We're working with the unconscious mind. In it, a whole realm of memories and experiences are stored. Remember, it is your friend and will only allow to surface what it sees to be appropriate and helpful to you.'

'OK.' I was dozing off already. *Friend, unconscious,* I thought as I listened to Fiona begin the familiar countdown. It wasn't long before I felt myself drifting in a timeless state of mind, rested to the point of falling asleep.

'You're going back,' Fiona, voice droned, 'back to when you were young . . .'

Images of my childhood flashed into my mind as she spoke. Gardens. Mum and Dad. Effy. I felt totally safe partly because the process had become familiar and partly because I trusted Fiona and what she said.

'If it's helpful, you could go back even further, back to a time before your birth. Before the time you returned to in our last session, to a time when you lived . . .'

I saw a tunnel, dark and faint, then a pale light, fog at the end. I tried to see further into it but felt I couldn't.

'You're feeling very calm and relaxed now. If it's appropriate you will go back. If the time's not right, you will still feel relaxed, calm, at ease.'

The mist began to clear. I could see a room. I felt small and cold.

'I see my mother,' I said. 'But she's not my mother from this life.'

'Who are you?'

'Me. Henrietta.' I said it with certainty this time. I wasn't trying. I knew I was her.

'And who is your mother?'

'Cecilia. She's sewing in the corner. I'm very happy. We're happy. Oh but, my father. He gets sick.'

Suddenly I felt wracked with grief.

'How old are you?'

'Eight. My dad works at the glassworks. He makes fancy glass bells. I take his supper to him when he's on nights.'

'What's your father's name?'

'Tom. My mum's got all dressed up for his funeral.'

I felt a terrible sadness. I didn't like what I was seeing. My dad being buried. It was cold, wet. My mother crying. Make it go away, make it go away.

Everything went grey, like a television screen that had lost its picture. I felt like I was drifting again then became aware of Fiona's voice. She sounded so far away. 'Where are you now, Jo?'

I felt uncomfortable and drifted away again. I started to feel myself relax, and the images began to reappear.

'What happened? Where are you?' Fiona asked.

'We went into the workhouse when I was nine, after my dad died. They put you out if you can't pay your rent. Our house was boarded up and we was thrown out.'

'Who went into the workhouse?'

'Me and me mam and John, my little brother. I had lovely black curly hair, but they cut it all off at the workhouse. Me mam's too. I don't like it here. My mam's in the washhouse scrubbing clothes, working hard cos you have to earn your keep. I feel awful. Bleak. Hopeless.'

The images seemed to be flitting about to different points in Henrietta's life, but I could see it all so clearly. I felt like I was describing a film but a film in which I had a starring role.

'I'm happy. I'm six. I'm at home with my dad and my mam. I love my dad very much. He's a good singer and always invited to weddings to sing.'

The images began to change and I felt older again.

'I'm fourteen at school in Macclesfield. The Industrial school. Oo it's such a beautiful place. I can count to ten on my fingers. One, two, three . . . I get prizes. One in Standard Four and another for darning. I'm a good darner.'

'What about your job in service?' Fiona coaxed.

The inner images seemed to fast-forward like on a DVD.

'I started as a mother's help. My lady has three children. It's at my lady's house where I met Katie Barrow.'

Katie Barrow. Inwardly, a jolt of recognition went through me. Shock at her memory. Katie. *Katie!* How could I have forgotten her all these years?

'Who's Katie?' Fiona asked.

'Golden-haired Katie they call her. She has this natural golden hair. She's knocked about by her dad. Katie is two years older than me but she's my friend and we're in service together.

'I send me mam money. She's in a poor way, drinking and that. My mind's worried. I can't sleep to think I'm comfortable and my mother . . . I send her money. I have a little bank book with about eight pounds which is a lot of money I've saved.'

The images seemed to fast-forward again and I desperately tried to keep up and make sense of what I was remembering.

'Do you want to continue, Jo?' Fiona asked.

I nodded. I felt totally relaxed and intrigued as if looking at a home movie I hadn't watched for a long time. 'Katie went down to London and she wrote me to come to join her. She's my best friend. She has beautiful clothes and a real china tea set. We share lodgings.' It was weird lying there, watching and remembering images that were so familiar but also so dream-like.

'Katie has a baby. It dies. We have no money to bury it. It has to go in a subscription grave. The undertaker says they took all the horses because there's a big funeral on, so we have to carry the baby to the cemetery. When we get to the church, they's burying someone else. There are big crowds. A big coffin for whoever's died and Katie's little one next to it on a little stool. The priest says prayers for the man that's died and then he turns to us. There's only me and Katie on our side and he says, we won't only pray for this little child, we'll pray for this mother that's lost him . . . Oh, when he says that we both burst out crying right from our very hearts.'

Intense grief wracked me and I found myself sobbing. It felt hopeless.

Far away, I heard Fiona's voice. 'Jo, Jo, it's all right . . . safe and easy . . . focusing on your breath, the feel of the couch beneath you, the sounds of the traffic outside . . .'

I felt myself coming back and followed Fiona's words.

'When you open your eyes, you'll feel . . .'

I was back in Fiona's office. I was safe but shivering. I felt so cold.

Fiona put a blanket over me. 'Are you all right?'

I took a few deep breaths. 'I'm fine. It was like the most vivid dream. I can see it all so clearly. So sad that Henrietta lost her father when she was young, just like me in this life. And Katie Barrow. I can't believe I'd forgotten about her.'

'Remarkable,' said Fiona as she switched off her recorder. 'Your recall was so articulate.'

'But where did all that come from?'

'You went very deep this time, Jo. Relax here for a while and take some deep breaths. Don't try and work it out or analyse too much. Let it settle.'

'Can I take the recording to listen to?'

'Yes of course you can. I'll do a copy for you. Now just relax.'

Easy to say, I thought as I closed my eyes. The

images had been so vivid and totally unexpected. Most of all, the memory of Katie was so strong. My dearest and closest friend. *How could I have forgotten her?* I asked myself.

Chapter Twenty-four

Even Effy was stuck for words after she'd heard the CD. I called her and Tash as soon as I'd left Fiona's and we all met at Effy's house where I played them the CD of the session.

'It was so weird,' said Tash. 'It was your voice all right but not how you speak or your language and how could you have known all those things?'

'I don't know. I did think maybe it was a film I'd seen, or something like that but. . .'

'What?' said Effy.

'It felt so real. There are a few details that we could check out, and if they turn out to be true, then I know for certain, it was no film I was recalling.'

'What details?'

'Henrietta's family. I said all of their names, her mum was Cecilia, her dad Tom and she had a younger brother John. I have a feeling that you or Tash mentioned those names to me when you first found the Gleesons on the census online so maybe I remembered them. We can double-check those.'

Tash nodded. 'I think you're right. I seem to remember we found a Cecilia.'

'But more importantly, there was one detail that has never appeared anywhere before: Katie Barrow and her baby. The first I knew about them was in my regression. I felt like I really knew her. As I say on the recording, she was my best friend. If Dave and his computer-whiz uncle can find her and maybe even a record of her child, then we know for definite that Betty didn't make the story up. She never mentioned Katie and neither did Lily, the other clairvoyant. That came from inside me and me alone.'

'Wow,' said Tash. 'You're right.'

'Maybe I was Katie,' said Effy.

'Or me,' said Tash.

'I thought about that,' I said. 'But don't you think Betty would have said something? She saw all of us that afternoon on the Heath.'

Effy nodded. 'Yeah maybe. But you did say that you felt I looked familiar the first time you met me and I felt the same about you.'

We looked at each other for a moment then both smiled. 'Maybe you were Katie,' I said. 'Maybe Tash was. Maybe I've known both of you before and maybe that's why Betty didn't say anything that afternoon on the Heath. She didn't need to because, unlike Howard and Henrietta, we've all found each other.'

Tash laughed. 'A lot of maybes there but hey, you could be right. *Maybe* we have been together loads of lifetimes.'

'What about Howard?' asked Effy.

'I didn't get to that part of Henrietta's life,' I said. 'I was younger, sometimes about nine, at times six, sometimes about fourteen, but all before she started working as a governess.'

'Will you have another session?'

'Definitely. I want to see what happened.'

'And you're OK with it?'

I shrugged. 'Yes. No. Fascinated more than anything. I feel that there's no going back now. If I don't go under again, I'm going to spend the rest of my life wondering about how Henrietta's life turned out. And Fiona is as intrigued as I am, she suggested we do another session. I just hope it helps answer some questions about *this* life too.'

Fiona fitted me in for another session on the Thursday of the same week.

'You really are an interesting case,' she said as she positioned her recorder ready for the session. 'Such recall. But don't be surprised if nothing happens this time. There are no guarantees and remember, the unconscious will only reveal what is most useful to you.'

'I know.'

I got settled on the couch and Fiona went through her usual countdown. This time though, I found it harder to relax and didn't seem to be drifting away.

'Where are you, Jo? Fiona asked after a while.

'Right here on the couch. You were right. It doesn't seem to be working this time.'

'Maybe you're trying too hard. Don't *try* to make it happen. Forget about Henrietta or trying to remember. Just let go and if we have a session purely for relaxation, that will be fine too. Do you want to take a break or carry on?'

Fiona's words reassured me. 'Let's carry on,' I said.

Fiona took me through a visualisation down through a wood, past water to a lake. I focused on her words and let my mind follow the images she was presenting. Down steps, through dappled sunlight. Soon I was drifting pleasantly, almost asleep when the internal misty TV screen appeared.

'Where are you, Jo?'

I focused on the mistiness. I felt alone. Sad.

'Katie's gone.'

'Gone where?' asked Fiona.

Suddenly the connection was there again. 'I don't want to go the way Katie has. She ran away from the big house where she was working cos she was having the baby. She had to. They put unmarried mothers into the asylum. And it weren't her fault. He said he'd look after her, the baby's father, but he never did. And now she can't get no references. When the baby died, she started drinking with her pals. Jugging it from six o'clock in the morning to eleven at night. Crowds of 'em. It was only a penny a gill. Oooooh she had a mouth on her when she'd been jugging it. She was never the same. No one ever called her golden-haired Katie any more, she were a wreck. She died soon after. They put German measles on the death certificate, but it wasn't German measles and I said so to the Inspector of the town. I said there should be an inquest but he said, what good's that. It won't bring her back. She were my friend, and now she were laid out. Such a beautiful girl, gone.'

I could see it clearly and didn't want to talk about it any more. I drifted for a while then more images came into view and I felt as if I was going forward in time.

I saw a house in a big garden with a wrought iron fence around it. I recognised the house. Detached, double-fronted, a bay window to the side and a brass sign to the left of the front door saying: *Edward Watts. Doctor*. There are fields opposite. I live there with the family. I feel a rush of excitement.

'Where are you now, Jo?' asked Fiona.

'In a kitchen. A lovely house. Bright from tall windows and it's warm. I've got a job and I'm dressed up and try to speak more refined. I look after Daniel. He's a baby. Daniel's got a cough and I've got a bottle of Scott's emulsion for him. I got it from the chemist's. And. . .'

A boy entered the room. He looked about nineteen. Just like when I saw Katie, I felt a jolt of recognition. It was like electricity going through me. Pure joy. It was Howard. My Howard. *It's been so long*, I thought. *He was my everything, my all. He occupied my every thought. I loved my job because every day I might see him in the garden, in the corridor, in the kitchen. Our eyes would meet, connect. It was our secret. How could I have forgotten him? He was my life.*

I felt bewildered. *Where have I been?* I asked myself. *I've been lost for years and years, forgotten what was most important. How could that have happened? I've been in a dream, a dream in which he hasn't featured. Where's he been? Where have I been?*

Howard's tall and dark with gentle, grey eyes that are looking at me, full of tenderness and longing. I'm happy just to be close to him. We're laughing at Daniel's face as he takes his cough mixture. He doesn't like it.

I feel a raw ache to be with him, an emptiness inside because I have been without him for so long, and am aware that tears are running down my cheeks.

I can't look any more. The craving to be with Howard is too overwhelming. I know, deep inside, that he's no more than an image from my unconscious mind, but that is what makes it unbearable. He's lost to me here and now, in this present time where I'm lying on a couch in Highgate remembering from some well deep inside of myself, a boy I should never have forgotten. Howard Watts. My soulmate.

But already his image is becoming shadowy and fading back into time gone by.

'Jo, Jo.' Fiona's voice pierced into my consciousness. 'Jo, Jo, you're coming back now and when you wake you'll be safe and relaxed . . .'

I focused on her voice, let myself be brought back and felt myself awakening.

'Waking up now, three, feeling at ease, calm, and two, when you open your eyes you will feel refreshed as though waking from a deep sleep, one.'

I opened my eyes. Back in Fiona's office. Back in the present day. But I had not forgotten.

Fiona let me lie for a few minutes before she spoke. *I won't forget*, I thought. *I mustn't.*

'The house where Henrietta worked,' I told Fiona. 'It was the house from my recurring dream.'

'And how do you feel about that, Jo?' she asked.

Another wave of loss flooded over me. Howard. I had seen his tombstone, his grave, and I could no longer reach him. He was gone from me, not just to another city or country but to another time. 'So much loss,' I said. *I don't know where to find Howard*, I thought with despair. *Henrietta lost her dad and I lost mine and now I've lost Howard.* I couldn't tell Fiona any more. It all felt so sad. As I lay there, suddenly a glimmer of hope flickered inside of me, growing stronger. If Betty was right and, like Henrietta, Howard is back too, then I have to find him. If we've come so far through time to be together then if there's even a chance we could be together, we must take it and never lose each other again.

Fiona took my hand. 'Are you OK?' She looked at me with concern and the touch of her hand was reassuring. 'You seem sad.'

'I saw him,' I told her. 'I saw Howard.'

Even saying his name cut into me. I felt panic. I didn't want to lose the memory of his face. I had no photograph, just an image in my mind that was already fading fast, like a candle about to burn out, flickering then dying, leaving me in the dark, desolate and alone.

'I'll be fine,' I said, but I was cold and shivering.

Fiona found a blanket and wrapped me in it like she had the time before. 'Lie quiet for a while,' she advised. 'It's a lot to absorb. Your unconscious mind needs to assimilate what you experienced.'

'It was so real,' I said, 'but already it's going, like waking from a dream.'

'Yes. You'll find that the vividness of the images will start to fade, but what's important will stay.'

She was right. Something important was still with me. The deep ache of loss and sense of urgency that I must find Howard.

The saying that it's better to have loved and lost than never to have loved at all went through my mind. *Not true*, I thought. *To have loved someone that intensely and lose them forever would be unbearable. Was everything that had happened in the last few weeks as a result of my and Howard's souls calling out to each other through ages of loneliness so that we could be together again?* I had to believe that it was so.

Chapter Twenty-five

Tash called with the news. Dave's uncle had found Katie.

Katie Barrow. Born Liverpool, 1880. Died Euston, London, 1900. German measles.

The details just as I'd recalled my session. He'd also found a Martha Barrow. Born 1898. Died 1898. Katie's baby.

After my last session with Fiona, I'd had no doubt that they'd find Katie Barrow. But Tash confirming the details made it all seem very real.

'Katie's story is so sad,' said Effy. 'It sounds like the father of her baby abandoned her or wouldn't own up to it. No wonder Henrietta didn't want to go the same way as her friend.'

'It would have been a scandal,' said Tash. 'The family that Henrietta worked for probably sent Howard away in the hope that he'd meet someone from his own class. Henrietta would have been considered beneath him.'

'Hey. Henrietta is back as Jo and hopefully Howard's around somewhere too,' said Effy, 'so why not Katie and the father of her baby as well? She could find him and give him a good slap!'

I laughed. 'Maybe it's a good job that people don't remember their past lives.'

Effy nodded. 'In one of the books I read about reincarnation, it said that when a person dies and a soul passes on, they are meant to forget their past life and start anew with a fresh slate. Sometimes though, something goes wrong with the passing over process which explains why some people have recall of their past life, like something didn't get sealed off or some memory bank wasn't emptied.'

'Whatever the explanation, what now, Jo?' asked Tash.

'I have to see it through,' I said. 'One hundred per cent definitely. I now have no doubt at all that what Betty told me was true. I was Henrietta and I have to find Howard. Nothing must come between us this time.'

Effy shook her head. 'I never *ever* thought I'd hear you say that.'

'Never say never,' I said.

Effy laughed. 'I won't.'

'So do you think it's Finn? Or Ben? Or even Owen?' asked Tash.

'Or someone I haven't met yet. I don't know. What if I don't meet him until I'm thirty or forty or fifty?'

'Did Betty not say?' asked Effy.

'No. Only that I must find him.'

'I don't think all this has come about now to lead nowhere or to make you wait ten years,' said Tash.

'Do you think everything that has happened has all been fate?' I asked. 'As if Betty being on the Heath that day set off a chain of events. If love is as predestined as that, it doesn't leave much room for choice.'

'I think you can choose in the end,' said Tash. 'These are different times to the Victorian age. Henrietta probably didn't meet a lot of boys. You, on the other hand, go to a mixed school, will go on to university, then get a job. You're going to meet lots of new people in this life, lots of new boys. You might even find Howard and decide you don't want him this time around.'

242

'I don't think so,' I said. 'There was such a power-ful connection.'

'In the meantime, Harry told us that whoever leaves flowers on the Watts grave will be back this Saturday,' said Effy. 'All we can do is follow each lead that we get, and that's the next one.'

'Agreed,' I said. 'And see where that takes us if anywhere.'

On Saturday morning, I was up early again. Mum had already gone to do the early shift at the hospital and I was grateful that she wasn't around to ask too many questions because I didn't have any answers.

Harry wasn't at the lodge when we got to the ceme-tery and the guide on duty didn't seem to know much about the regulars who came to lay flowers.

'So what do we do?' asked Tash as we went back to the gate.

'We wait,' I said.

'We might be here all day,' said Tash.

'I guess we just have to hope that whoever it is, is an early bird,' I replied.

A small crowd gathered for the ten o'clock tour but no-one was carrying flowers and they all looked liked tourists.

After they'd gone inside, a man in his forties appeared, carrying a bunch of carnations and roses. Although Harry had said that it was a lady who came to lay flowers, I wasn't going to leave anything to chance.

'Excuse me, but are you going to the Watts grave?' I asked.

'No I'm not,' he said and gave me a look as if to say, mind your own business.

'What are we going to say if it is the right person?' I asked Effy as the man disappeared inside. 'We'd better get our story straight or we might upset whoever it is. We can't tell the truth as they'll think we're mad. And if we say we know the Watts family, they might ask how?'

'We could say we're distant relatives of Henrietta,' Effy suggested, 'and we knew that she'd worked as a governess and discovered who the family were from the census records.'

It sounded reasonable enough.

A lady in her twenties arrived next. She got out of a car further down the lane and walked towards us carrying a bunch of pink flowers. She had dark hair and I felt my pulse begin to race. Could this be the woman we wanted? Or was she too young?

This time, Effy approached her. 'Excuse me but are you going to the Watts grave?'

She shook her head and looked more friendly than the man earlier. 'No,' she replied. 'Parkinson. My grandfather.' She looked over at the gate. 'It's a fabulous place, isn't it?'

Effy nodded as the lady walked on.

No-one came for another couple of hours apart from the groups of tourists arriving for the hourly tours. I was beginning to get bored and storm clouds were gathering. I felt bad for making Tash and Effy stand outside a cemetery all morning.

'I'll go and get some warm drinks to keep us going,' I said.

Effy nodded. 'Need chocolate too,' she said.

I set off towards the village, but I hadn't gone far when I spotted an elderly woman with white hair coming down the lane towards me. She was carrying a bunch of small white flowers. *Could this be her?* I thought as I turned back to join Tash and Effy.

As the woman got closer I realised that it was Mrs Rayner, the lady who volunteers at Mum's hospital. She glanced over at us and her face lit up when she saw me. 'Is that Jo?' she asked and came towards us.

'Hi, Mrs Rayner,' I said. 'How are you doing?'

'Good, thanks.' She looked at Tash and Effy. 'What are you girls doing here? Have you done the tour?'

'Yes, we have. It's amazing in there,' I said. 'Um, these are my friends Tash and Effy.'

'Hi,' they chorused.

'Are you going in?' I asked.

Mrs Rayner indicated the flowers. 'Yes.'

'You're not by any chance going to the Watts grave, are you?' I asked.

'Why yes. How did you know?'

I suddenly felt nervous and my well-concocted story deserted me. I so didn't expect that the person we were waiting for would be someone I knew. 'I, er . . .'

'How did you know?' she asked again, her grey eyes boring into me.

'I, er . . . I knew Henrietta, well, not exactly knew her, knew of her.'

'Henrietta? Who's Henrietta?' asked Mrs Rayner.

'She was the Wattses's governess.'

'Governess? What are you talking about, Jo?'

'Sorry. Henrietta. She was governess to the Watts family at the turn of the nineteenth century . . . I think.'

Effy could see that I was struggling and took over. 'I can explain,' she said. 'I realise that this must look strange but we're not nutters. We've been doing some

246

research into Jo's family tree and found a lady called Henrietta. We found out on the census records that she was governess to the Watts family. We visited the cemetery to find the Watts family grave, and Harry, who works at the front lodge, said that someone came and laid flowers on the grave on this date and a few weeks before every year.'

'That's right, I do.' said Mrs Rayner. 'On my father's anniversary and then my grandmother's.'

'I'm sorry if it sounds mad but we were intrigued to find out who was leaving the flowers. We couldn't help ourselves so came back to see if we could find out who it was and if, maybe, they knew anything about Henrietta,' I said.

Mrs Rayner considered the story for a moment. 'I see. So you've been researching a family tree. So this Henrietta, she was an aunt or grandmother?'

'Great-great-aunt,' I lied. 'She never married.'

'So what is it you wanted to know from me?' asked Mrs Rayner.

'If you might know anything about the family or Henrietta or Ho— or any of them,' I said.

'Yes I do,' said Mrs Rayner. 'Daniel Watts was my father.'

'No way,' I blurted.

'I think I know who my father was,' said Mrs Rayner with a smile. 'My maiden name is Watts.'

'There were two children, weren't there?' asked Effy. 'In the Watts household?'

Mrs Rayner nodded. 'Daniel and his brother Howard. How did you know?'

'Er . . . We saw the inscriptions on the grave,' said Effy. 'I guessed that Howard might have been Daniel's brother.'

'From letters, diaries she left,' Tash said at the same time as Effy.

'How very interesting,' said Mrs Rayner. 'So what do you know about this Henrietta?'

'Not much,' I said. 'We know that she was born in Manchester and that her father died when she was young. She worked in service and later became a governess. She would have looked after Daniel, your father, I think. She died at a young age.'

'We'd love to find out more,' said Effy.

Mrs Rayner considered what I'd said. 'I may be able to help you there. I have my father's photograph albums and I believe there are a few that are from that time. They're mainly of family, but there were some of my father when he was very young with his brother Howard. If I remember rightly there's a young lady there in a couple of them, dark-haired. I knew she wasn't family and she looked too well turned out for a housemaid. I've always wondered who she was. She must have been your Henrietta.'

'Ohmigod,' I blurted. 'Do you think we could come and see them?' I clapped my hand over my mouth. 'Sorry. I mean, I'd . . . we'd quite understand if you say no.'

Mrs Rayner smiled. 'Of course you can. I can see that this governess has captured your imaginations and . . . now she's captured mine. You see, my father died many years ago and there was so much I wished I'd asked him about his life before he passed away but I do remember a little of what he said about his early youth. You'd be very welcome to come and see what I have.'

'Can we come today?' I asked.

Mrs Rayner smiled. 'Why not? No time like the present,' she said. 'Wait for me here while I go and put the flowers on my father's grave and I'll take you back with me.'

As she went into the cemetery, I let out a long breath of air.

'Amazing,' said Effy.

'I know,' I said, 'an incredible coincidence.'

'Synchronicity,' said Effy.

'Which is?' I asked.

'It's when there's a connection between something going on outside and something happening inside you. It might look like coincidence or fate or destiny.'

'So you're saying this whole thing is fate?'

Effy nodded. 'Your destiny making itself clear.'

'But it isn't, is it?' said Tash. 'I mean, if it was clear then it would be obvious who Jo should pick, but right now she doesn't know. It could be Ben or Finn.'

'Or Owen, don't forget Owen,' said Effy. 'Often true love starts with friendship.'

Tash wrinkled up her nose. 'I think it's the other way around. I think there's an almighty attraction and then friendship grows out of that.'

I rolled my eyes. 'Well that's a lot of help. You two can't agree on anything.' I looked over in the direction of the cemetery. 'Do you realise what we've found out today – that Mrs Rayner is the daughter of the small boy I held in my arms in a previous life. And yet, here she is, loads older than me. She's also Howard's niece. How totally mad is that? Maybe she can tell us what happened to him. What he was like. And not only that, we're going to get to see a photograph of them.' I really hoped so because the image of

Howard from my hypnotherapy session was fading and I was finding it hard to hang on to what he looked like. Other faces were taking precedence. Sometimes Finn's, sometimes Ben's and sometimes Owen's.

I couldn't wait until Mrs Rayner returned.

Chapter Twenty-six

We set off eagerly with Mrs Rayner, who had parked her car up the lane. Effy got into the front and chatted away to her while Tash and I sat in the back.

'You OK, Jo?' whispered Tash.

'Oh yes. I can't wait to see the photos. Like, if the consciousness, soul, spirit, whatever you want to call it, that's inside of me is the same as was in Henrietta, then it would be the same with Howard and whoever he is now too.'

'I don't understand,' said Tash. 'What are you saying?'

'Mum always says that the eyes are the window of the soul. So maybe I'll see something in the photographs of Howard, a spark or a spirit in his eyes that might help me recognise who he is today.'

'That would be so amazing,' said Tash.

'Exactly,' I said.

Mrs Rayner drove up to the village, turned right down the High Street then left into one of the smaller roads. I knew Highgate well having lived nearby for most of my life but I'd never been down the maze of side streets here before. Like so many roads in the area, there were houses from different eras. Mrs Rayner drove into a cul-de-sac with a row of modern terraces on the right and properties dating back to Victorian and Edwardian times on the left.

She drove to the end of the road and parked. When we got out, I could see a tall wooden fence on the side with the old houses. In the middle of the fence was a tall gate with a rose arch over it. Number twenty-four.

'Here we are,' said Mrs Rayner as she unlatched the gate. 'Come on in.'

We followed her through and I took a sharp intake of breath. I knew the house immediately. Detached, double-fronted, set back from the road with a large garden on three sides and a bay window to the right. It was the house from my dream and the house I'd seen in my regression. The house that Henrietta had lived and worked in.

Mrs Rayner and Effy went up the steps to the front door while I held back for a moment. I felt suddenly faint.

'What is it, Jo?' asked Tash. 'You've gone pale.'

'I know this place,' I whispered. 'But how? On the census, it said that the Watts family lived at Halville House, Trafalgar Road. We'd looked it up in the A–Z and couldn't find it, remember?' I looked around me as Mrs Rayner fumbled in her bag to find her keys up on the porch with Effy. 'When I saw it in my regression, those houses at the bottom of the garden, over the fence, they weren't there, and there were no houses opposite where that modern terrace is now. There was nothing but fields for miles and miles, but the house . . .' There was no mistaking it despite the changes. 'There was a wrought iron fence all around where the wooden fence is now and,' I pointed to the middle of the garden, 'a fountain there.'

'Do you want to go home?' asked Tash. 'Are you up to this?'

'You're kidding! Get this close and go home? No way. I'll be fine. It's just weird, I've never been here before, but I recognise it so well.'

'Come on in, girls,' said Mrs Rayner as she opened

the front door and beckoned us forward. 'I'll put the kettle on then find those photos for you.'

We followed her into the hall. 'But where are the stairs?' I blurted as I looked around. I could remember exactly how it used to look, with dark green walls covered with gold-framed landscapes, and there had been stairs up to the right with polished wooden banisters.

Effy threw me a 'shut up' glance but luckily Mrs Rayner just seemed to assume that in a house like this, it was obvious there would have been stairs at one time.

'Oh, they were taken out years ago,' she said, 'when the house was converted to flats. Luckily I was able to keep my front door. The entrance to the upstairs flat is round the side.' She ushered us into a sitting room to the left. It was full of dark old furniture.

'Do sit down,' said Mrs Rayner as she indicated a sofa by the fireplace.

'I like your antique furniture,' I said as I took a seat.

'Thank you, Jo,' said Mrs Rayner. 'I inherited the furniture from my parents along with the house. It was a grand old place before the conversion but too big for them and the ground-floor flat suited them better when they grew older, as it suits my needs now. I wouldn't know what to do with floors of empty rooms. Now I'll go and put that kettle on.' She disappeared out into the hall and moments later, we could hear the clattering of cups and saucers coming from the back of the house.

As I looked around, I had a strange sensation of past and present merging, like on house makeover shows on TV when you see an image of a room before it's decorated and then it flashes to the finished version. In my mind's eye, I could see the room as it had been but I was looking at it as it was today.

'This used to be the dining room,' I said to Tash and Effy. 'It had deep red walls and a long polished mahogany table in the middle of the room.'

'Wow. I wish I could see it how it was,' said Tash. 'Sounds amazing.'

Mrs Rayner reappeared with a tray which she put down on the coffee table in front of us.

'So you want to know more about your great-aunt?' she said after she'd poured us tea and offered us slices of yummy cherry cake. 'I have a vague recollection of my father talking about her. I'll get the album. It's just in here, in the cabinet.'

She got up and rooted around in the large piece of furniture in the corner. 'Here we are,' she said as she pulled an album from a lower cupboard. She put it on the table in front of us and flicked through until she found the page she was looking for. It was a lovely old-fashioned book and each of the photos had been placed in a delicate paper frame of painted leaves and flowers. She pointed to a sepia photograph on the right-hand page.

'There she is, I think,' she said.

I looked down and Effy and Tash moved closer so that they could see as well.

There she was. Henrietta Gleeson. A young woman with dark curly hair smiling out at us from the faded sepia photograph. It had been taken in the garden and she was standing under an apple tree holding a toddler, a chubby boy in a sailor suit.

'She's beautiful!' Effy exclaimed.

'Must run in the family,' said Mrs Rayner as she looked at me. 'I can see a resemblance around the eyes.'

I felt myself blush deep red and continued to stare at the photograph. I searched the face looking for what Mrs Rayner saw around the eyes but I could see no resemblance myself. It felt eerie to consider that I was once this person. A woman older than I am now. In a different body. I shivered. I wondered what she was really like. From my regression, I knew that she hadn't had an easy life. I hoped that she'd found some happiness with the Watts family. With Howard.

Mrs Rayner pointed at the toddler. 'That's my father,' she said. 'He must have been about two in that photograph.' She flicked over to the next page. 'Here are some more from that time.'

I looked at the top photograph. 'Howard!' I blurted and I pointed to a boy in the shot. There was no mistaking him. He was the boy I'd seen in my regression, and seeing his picture, all the feelings I'd felt when under hypnosis came rushing back. He was pictured with his family – a formal portrait with his father standing next to him and his mother seated with Daniel on her knee. In the background was Henrietta, her expression this time serious. *Poor Henrietta*, I thought, *to have been so in love with him but not able to truly be with him.*

'Hey, he was handsome,' said Tash.

'How did you know that is my uncle?' asked Mrs Rayner as Effy shot me another warning glance.

'Oh! A good guess,' I said. 'We saw the names on the grave . . . you know, at the cemetery.'

Mrs Rayner paused for a few moments. 'Oh, yes.'

'Did you know him?' asked Tash.

Mrs Rayner shook her head. 'He died long before I was born. I'd like to have known him though. My father talked about him very fondly. He looks like he was a nice fellow, doesn't he?'

'Er . . . Mrs Rayner, you said you remembered some talk of Henrietta. Can you remember what was said?' I asked.

'Some scandal to do with a governess, I believe.' She came back over and pointed to Henrietta in the photo. 'I didn't know her name, but I've always thought it must have been her because later ones looked much older. Yes, that was it, the young governess was dismissed and Howard was sent away to Europe. My father said he missed him dreadfully and made such a fuss that Howard was allowed to come back after a few years. I seem to remember my father saying that the young governess had been dismissed by then and replaced by a series of older women. I don't think he was very keen on any of them. Apparently my grand-mother believed that Howard could make a better marriage. It wasn't done in those days to have relations with servants, even if she was a governess. But Howard never did marry.'

So that's what Betty had meant when she'd said some-thing had happened to keep them apart, I thought. I felt so sad for them both but Howard had been there when Henrietta was dying so he had clearly found her again at some point.

Mrs Rayner flicked through to later photographs showing a slightly older Daniel with his parents and a stern-faced woman in the background. She laughed. 'I think this was the next governess,' she said. 'I can't imagine Howard ever having fallen for her, can you? She looks a bit of a battleaxe, doesn't she?'

I looked at one of the images in front of me. A thin-lipped, middle-aged lady held Daniel on her knee. He didn't look happy.

'What happened to Henrietta?' I asked.

'After she was dismissed? That I don't know,' said Mrs Rayner.

'She died young,' said Tash. 'We saw it on her grave. Aged twenty-three.'

'How sad,' said Mrs Rayner. 'She looked a nice young lady too. They would have made a handsome couple but then things were different in those days.' She flicked through some more pages to show more family photos but no others showing Henrietta. 'My grandfather Edward died before I was born so I never met him. Howard died in the First World War, he was very young.' She got up to look in the cabinet. 'I believe I have his death certificate somewhere. There's a whole pile of papers, letters and documents from that time. I haven't looked at them in years. Let me see what I can find.'

'Do you have children, Mrs Rayner?' asked Tash.

'I do. Two girls. A daughter who lives in New Zealand now and the other lives in south London. She has three children, a boy and two girls. So yes, the Watts family has gone on.' She continued her search in the cabinet. 'Sadly not the family house though. It has been through many changes.' She pulled out a box. 'Ah, here we are.'

'Do you know when the name of the road changed from Trafalgar to Northern?' asked Tash. 'When we looked on the census, it said Halville House, Trafalgar Road.'

'Ah, that was around the nineteen-sixties. This end of the road was always Trafalgar Road but when the area became more built up, they extended the road down to meet the main street so it made sense to have one name rather than two for the two different ends and so it became Northern Road.'

'And when was the house made into flats?' I asked.

'Around the same time. So sadly I can't show you where Henrietta would have had her room but I can show you where she would have worked on this floor. Would you like to have a look?'

'We'd love to,' Effy answered for me.

As we went around, the memories of how the house used to look kept flashing in my mind, sharp and clear. What was now Mrs Rayner's bedroom, decorated in pale blue and white, had been a dark and formal parlour with heavy curtains at the bay window. The kitchen had been extended and modernised, but I could see it as it was with an old-fashioned stove, open shelves of pots and pans, and memories of a cook, always busy preparing something. There also used to be a balcony that looked out over the garden but it was gone and a sunny conservatory built in its place. It was extraordinary to have so many clear memories of a place which I was visiting for the first time.

Mrs Rayner offered more tea after our tour but we felt it was time to leave so declined her offer and said our goodbyes.

'Leave me your number, Jo,' she said to me. 'And I'll give you a call if I find anything else. I fancy I might have a root through all the papers for a few hours now that I've got them out. You never know what's in there.'

I wrote my landline number down for her and then we left.

'So now we know more about Henrietta,' said Effy as we stood outside for a moment and looked back at the house. 'But still no closer to finding Howard if he's back in this time too.'

'Yeah,' I agreed. My head was spinning with the enormity of it all. 'Henrietta's room was there, up in the attic,' I said as I pointed at the top floor. 'You used to be able to see St George's in the distance – there were fields and hedgerows for miles where now there are rows and rows of houses.' I pointed down the road. 'There was a big manor house in parkland to the left where that row of terraced houses is. And another big house at the end of the road. Lynton Grange, that was it.'

As we walked back to the high street, the memories continued to flood in as if it had only been yesterday. 'There was a small cottage in the grounds of the Grange. It was where the vet lived. I remembered taking an assortment of kittens down there to see him. The wood to the back of the house was called

Dirt House Wood and at night, soil men used to put excrement there that they had collected from cesspits from a row of nearby cottages.'

'Are you making this up?' asked Effy.

I laughed. 'No. I promise.'

'It seems amazing that you remember so much,' said Effy. 'I mean, I get that you remembered the house but now you're teasing us.'

'I'm not. Honest. I can just see it.'

Effy and Tash exchanged a glance that said, yeah right.

'See that Barclays Bank at the corner of the road? It used to be Park Hall, the grandest house in the area. The pub over the road, the Bald Faced Stag? That was there when I was Henrietta but it was a coaching inn.'

Tash burst out laughing. 'Stop it, Jo. Now we definitely know you're making it up.'

I laughed. It appeared that we'd swapped roles since that day back on the Heath when I first met Betty. Then I'd thought the whole Henrietta story was baloney but Effy and Tash had felt there was something in it. Now they were the ones who didn't know what to believe and I had no doubts whatsoever.

'Thing is, Howard could be anywhere,' said Tash with a long sigh.

'I know,' I said. 'We found so much – the census records, the grave, the house and even photos of Howard and Henrietta – but we're no closer to finding Howard than we were that day on the Heath.'

'Well one thing has changed. You believe it's all true now,' said Effy, 'whereas back then you didn't.'

'I know, and sadly, that makes it all feel worse,' I said. 'In accepting the story, I also accept that I have lost the great love of my life – or should I say lives.'

The skies darkened and moments later, rain began to splash down on the streets. *Exactly how I feel*, I thought as we made a dash for a bus shelter.

Chapter Twenty-seven

When I got home, I threw my jacket off and glanced in the hall mirror. I had the sensation of Henrietta staring back at me again. *Haunted by myself*, I thought. I looked again. She'd gone. It was Jo Harris staring back at me.

'That you, Jo?' Mum called from the kitchen.

'Yep,' I called back. I was about to dash upstairs when she appeared in the hall. She didn't look happy.

'So when were you going to tell me what's going on?' she asked. 'I've just had Mrs Rayner on the phone.'

'Oh. What did she want?' I asked, trying to sound casual.

Mum beckoned me to follow her into the kitchen. I went in and sat at the table. Mum didn't sit. 'She wanted to tell you something she'd found out about a great-aunt you've been researching,' she said and gave me a quizzical look. 'What aunt would that be exactly?'

I felt myself blush and stared at the floor. Mum was quiet for a few moments, waiting for me to say something, but I didn't know where to begin.

Finally Mum sighed and sat down opposite. 'What were you doing hanging around the cemetery? And who's Howard? And Henrietta?' I glanced up at Mum and saw that her face looked concerned. 'Are you in trouble, Jo?'

'No!' As I looked at her worried face, I could see the kindness in her eyes and felt sudden tears at the back of mine. *Why had I shut her out for so long? I asked myself. Had I unconsciously blamed her for Dad's death? Or been angry with her that she couldn't fix it and keep him well and alive? Before Dad died, I used to chat away to her about everything, tell her all my secrets.*

She reached out and took my hand. 'You can tell me anything, Jo. I am always here for you.'

'I'm not in trouble, Mum. Nothing like that.' I took a deep breath and told her the whole story, right from the start and the day on the Heath to earlier that day at Mrs Rayner's. It felt good to talk it all out from beginning to end so that I could make sense of it too.

Mum listened quietly, not commenting. At one point, she got up and got us a glass of orange juice each from the fridge. When I'd finished, she got up, came over to me and gave me a big hug. It felt good to breathe in her familiar Mum smell and be wrapped in her arms. 'Oh, Jo, what a lot to have been carrying around with you.'

'There was nothing you could have done,' I said when she let me go.

'All the same, I wish you'd told me earlier,' she said as she sat back down.

'But there was nothing to tell or at least not until recently. It didn't make sense and I didn't believe it anyway, then as more things came to light, it all got so mixed up in my head, I didn't know what to think or say. You have to admit, it's kind of a mad story.'

'Yes but then what do we know about anything? After your dad died, I thought a lot about what happens next, like, where did he go? Does it end when the body dies? Who knows? I certainly don't. Here we all are and yet no-one really knows where we've come from, what we're doing here and where we go when the body wears out.'

'I know ... I mean, I don't know. I find it

overwhelming how *much* I don't know,' I said. 'It's *vast* how much I don't know!'

Mum looked at me tenderly. 'My little Jo. I hate to think you've been so unhappy these last weeks, trying to soldier on all by yourself under the weight of all this, but then, I suppose that's who you are or who you've become. You were so brave when your dad died. So determined to be strong.'

'I didn't want to upset you any more than you already were.'

Mum reached out and took my hand again. 'You'd just lost your father, Jo. You didn't need to hold it together for me. Maybe that recurring dream you've been having is because you didn't let it out.'

I felt my eyes fill with tears again. 'I don't think my dream was just about Dad. Henrietta lost her father at a young age too and then lost Howard. So much loss. My dad, her dad and now Howard.' I started to sob and soon the tears wouldn't stop. It felt like a floodgate inside me had opened and wave upon wave of pain and sadness burst forward. I wasn't even sure who I was crying for. For me or Mum or Howard or Henrietta or Dad. Mum was at my side in an instant and held me to her, her eyes also full of tears.

When I'd finally stopped, Mum let me go again and got me some tissues.

'So what did Mrs Rayner want?' I asked after I'd blown my nose.

'She called to say she'd found Henrietta's death certificate. It was amongst Howard's papers. The cause of death was tuberculosis. She said you might like to know.'

'Cause of Henrietta's death. My death. Major weird, don't you think?'

Mum nodded. 'Major. Though sometimes you have to accept there are some things we just don't understand. All I do know is that while we have this life, we must appreciate what's around us. Don't miss any of it. The cycles and recycles of nature. The way leaves change colour and fall in the autumn leaving the trees stripped and bare, like skeletons, the end of a cycle. Then out of nowhere come buds and the branches are full of blossom and new green leaves – it's like magic. Perhaps nature is telling us that is how it is on many levels. A constant renewal. Death leads to rebirth.'

'Do you think?' I asked as Mum stared out of the window as if deep in thought.

'When I was younger,' Mum continued, 'I was so sure about many things, so opinionated. As I've got older, I've realised that I know nothing for sure.'

I nodded. 'Do you think I might have been Henrietta?'

'Why not? It could be that you have some psychic power and have tuned into something that took place. There are people who have that gift, you know. On the other hand, maybe you were her. Why not? Either way though, she's gone. Died of tuberculosis. But you're still here as Jo, right here, right now, breathing and alive.'

'So you're saying live for the present and forget the past?'

'Not exactly. We all carry our past within us but don't dwell on it. It's gone. And I'm not saying don't have your plans for the future either. It's good to have goals. I'm just saying in the meantime, don't miss your life. Don't be so busy trying to work it all out that you miss the small stuff that's going on around you. Try to live in the present and enjoy all that there is to experience.'

'Sounds good,' I said.

'Do you have any idea which of the boys your Howard might be this time around?' asked Mum.

I shook my head. 'Not really. Maybe. I was hoping that seeing his photograph might shed some light but it didn't. And I was hoping that Mrs Rayner might be

271

able to tell us if he and Henrietta met up again between her dismissal and her death but she didn't know.'

'Maybe you have to let that go,' said Mum. 'If what you saw was right, then Howard was there at the end with her. You can't relive that life. It's gone and even though you have some of her memories, Henrietta wasn't the real you, Jo. The real you is in this century. You're a different person now in a different time with different options and choices to make. Yes, your Howard might be out there somewhere but meeting him might be down to the right timing. I am sure if your dad and I had met years earlier than we did, we wouldn't have hit it off at all. So maybe you'll meet your Howard when the time's right.'

'Maybe, though I hope I don't have to wait too long. When I saw him in the regression and then his photograph today at Mrs Rayner's, I felt like I really missed him, like an ache inside of me.'

Mum nodded and she looked sad for a moment. I knew she was thinking about Dad.

'But you know what, Mum? You're right about living for the present and enjoying your life and do you know what I feel like doing more than anything?'

'What's that, love?'

'I think in order to move on, I have to let go of the past and live right now, in the present, and I want to make some changes.'

Mum raised an eyebrow. 'Sounds exciting. So what are you going to do?'

'A makeover! Starting with my bedroom.'

Chapter Twenty-eight

'When you looked at the photo of Howard, Jo,' said Tash as she helped me take the posters down from my wall, 'did you see anything in the eyes? Anything that you feel would help you recognise him now?'

I shook my head. 'Not really. He looked intelligent and kind but it might be hard to recognise him now with a different face.'

'He might recognise you,' said Tash. 'Ever considered that?'

'That could make things easier,' I said.

'Your heart will recognise him and tell you who is right for you,' Tash continued. 'I don't think you need to worry too much. Love will find you.'

'I think it's Finn,' said Effy.

'Maybe. But he's such a flirt with everyone.'

'It could be because he was an unmarried Victorian gent in his last life,' said Effy. 'He's making up for it this time around.'

'I think it's Ben,' said Tash. 'From what you've told us about him, it sounds like he's got more depth than Finn.'

'And Owen is still there in the background, Jo,' added Effy. 'Don't rule him out. Feelings change and you know he'd always be there for you in a flash if you ever needed him.'

'I do,' I said. 'But it's not clear about any of them.' I knew that was a lie though. I felt that it had to be Finn. He was the one who occupied my thoughts and made my stomach flip but I didn't want to let on just how much I really liked him in case I ended up looking like a fool. 'Boys do my head in. A few weeks ago, I thought there were maybe three contenders for Howard and now, maybe none. Finn hasn't emailed me since the day after my party so for all I know, he's got off with some new girl he's met. And even if I did like Ben, I reckon I've blown it with him because he knows I'm so into his mate, and Owen, well it's on a different level with him. He's a mate but . . . maybe it was bad timing with us and I met the right guy at the wrong time.'

'You should tell each of them the whole story and see how they react,' said Effy. 'Though Owen already knows most of it.'

'I already know that Ben thinks that clairvoyants and past life stuff is tosh,' I said. 'And Finn would try and see how he could make it work for him. Like when I was going to see the clairvoyants for the magazine, he asked me to see if they said anything about him.'

Effy laughed. 'He's such a smoothie,' she said.

'But surely the right one will listen and understand and your story will resonate with him,' said Tash.

'Yeah,' said Effy. 'Tash is right. Maybe they've been experiencing synchronicity or recurring dreams of their own.'

'Yeah,' Tash agreed. 'Both Finn and Ben were there on the Heath that day Betty told you about Howard, and even weirder, so was Mrs Rayner. That was a coincidence too.'

'But you have to choose which boy in the end,' said Effy.

Betty's words came back to me. She had said exactly that: *You must choose.*

'But how do I decide?'

'Spend time with them,' said Tash.

'No. It's easier than that,' said Effy. 'Remember what you said about Owen. About how kissing him felt bland. No spark. What you need to do is snog them. You'll know then.'

I laughed. 'Effy, surely it can't be that straightforward? Not that black or white? And anyhow, what am I going to say? I need to kiss you to see if you're my soulmate from a past life? No. The moment has to be right. The feelings have to be there and as you just said, feelings change. I'm going to see what happens, and if it's meant to be, then it will be.'

Effy pouted. 'Oh, suit yourself then. Do it your way. Life is what you make it.'

'Excuse me, madam. What happened to fate, destiny, synchronicity? No. I'm going to trust that whatever's unfolded so far hasn't finished the job yet. No. It's not over by a long way.'

'Kiss them. Like the fairy tale, the frog will become the prince,' said Tash. 'The right boy will reveal himself to be Howard.'

I had to laugh. It was so simple to Tash. 'Listen, guys, we don't know if Henrietta even got to kiss Howard. What if she did and discovered there was no real spark there? Or she kissed him and they'd both lived and got bored with each other? You know how kisses can change. In the beginning, when you first like a boy, there's such a build-up of feelings that it's always good to start with. Then you get to know each other, find out if you get on. It can change. I don't think kissing Finn or Ben is the answer.'

'Coward,' said Effy. 'At the very least, it might eliminate one of them.'

'I think I should kiss a lot of boys. I mean, I'm seventeen. I haven't exactly had a lot of experience. Maybe I need some comparisons so that when I do kiss The One, I'll know it.'

'No, no,' said Tash. 'If either boy is Howard then it will be fireworks when you kiss him. I mean, you haven't waited weeks to get together. You've waited over a century! It will be magic.'

'You are such a romantic, Tash,' I said.

'I notice that you don't talk so much about Owen as a contender,' said Effy.

'I'm sorry, Effy, but much as I like him, love him even, I don't think I *love* love him,' I said. It was hard to say to Effy because of course, she wanted her brother to be happy, but my gut feeling was that if

Howard was Owen, I'd be disappointed. I was more with Tash and the idea that if I did find Howard, it would feel amazing. 'Even though I know I want someone special who feels the same way about me, I also know I can't force it. I can't make someone love me and I'm not going to make myself believe that I have to love someone just because I might have known them in a different life. Finn might be Howard. Ben might be Howard. Another boy might be Howard, and in this life maybe he's moved on, evolved, grown, and I might not be part of his journey this time. I have to accept that too.' I remembered what Mum had said about me after I'd told her the story. 'And I'm not Henrietta any more. I am Jo Harris with memories from this life as well as any past ones.'

'Except Betty said Howard is your soulmate and that you must find him,' said Tash. 'I don't think that will change. Sounds to me like whatever happens, you still have unfinished business with each other.'

I couldn't argue with that.

The next day, I went back to Fiona for my usual Monday appointment to see if anything more would come to light in another session, maybe some more interaction between Howard and Henrietta. Nothing did. I went into a light trance and felt relaxed but there was no regression of any kind.

'As I said to you in the beginning, Jo,' Fiona explained, 'the unconscious tends to throw up what is appropriate. In our previous sessions, I've no doubt that you went back to the moment of trauma, the loss that has caused your trouble sleeping. Now that has been isolated and confronted, there is no need to go back.'

It was true. Since the last session with Fiona and my big cry with Mum, I'd been sleeping like a baby and my recurring dream seemed to have disappeared. I felt disappointed that I wasn't able to go back to any further scenes with Howard though I told myself that was all the more reason I should find him in the present day.

In the meantime, I felt like I'd bonded with Mum again and we'd had a fun time looking at paint samples and soft furnishings, and soon after had begun work on my room. The girls helped me paint it a pale ivory on three walls and a pale powder blue on the other. Mum bought me a set of silver-grey curtains and once they were up, the whole room looked transformed, fresh and light.

'What about some pictures for the wall?' asked Mum.

'Not sure yet,' I said. 'I'm still looking.'

At the weekend, I took my birthday money and went shopping. I bought a pretty summer dress, knee length with tiny flowers in cornflower blue and coral, and a pair of strappy sandals to match. To complete the look, I booked into the hairdresser and had my hair cut to shoulder length with soft layers around the front. It felt like one of Effy's rituals, symbolising the end of the old Jo and the beginning of the new me.

'Wow,' chorused Effy and Tash when they came to meet me at my house after the hairdresser's.

'You look amazing,' said Tash.

I did a twirl. I felt amazing too – as if a dark cloud that I'd been carrying around with me for years had gone. Whether it was finally opening up to my mum about Dad or whether it was because I was learning to let go of Henrietta and her past, I didn't know. The only thing that was still bugging me was my part of the article I had to write for *Chillaxin*. Effy had done her side of it – explaining about the theory of reincarnation and including some stories from the books about past life experiences. I was supposed to take the opposite angle so that both points of view would be represented. However, I didn't feel that I could honestly write that it was all nonsense any more.

When Effy and Tash had gone, I made myself go upstairs, sat at my computer and stared at the blank page. I read and reread my notes from the visits to the different clairvoyants. In the end, I called Effy to complain that I didn't know what to say.

'Tell the truth,' she said. 'Whatever, just make a start. You can always change it later.'

I put down the phone and wrote up descriptions of the people we'd visited, what they looked like and what their homes felt like. I didn't put in the whole truth, more half the truth, omitting the parts about me, Henrietta and Howard.

When I'd finished, I emailed it through to Finn. An email came a short time later.

Hey Mary Poppins.

I thought you were taking the opposing view. What's changed? Let's meet tomorrow am to talk it through and where we want to go with this.

Finn

I read it a few times. Where we want to go with this? I was sure he meant us, not just the article, and a shiver of excitement went through me.

Chapter Twenty-nine

I blow-dried my hair until it shone, put a little eye make-up on, not too much as I didn't want him to think I'd tried too hard. A slick of lipgloss, a squirt of my Jicky perfume and I was ready. It was a lovely day so I decided to wear my new dress and a little red cardigan to go with it.

Finn was already there when I got to Costa and he glanced up at me when I went in, then did a double take as he didn't recognise me at first.

'Wow,' he said as I joined him at his table. 'You look different.'

'New century, new me,' I said.

'New century?'

'Er . . . I mean new, um . . . new look.'

He looked me up and down. 'Nice. I mean, I liked the old you. I liked that Victorian style, it kind of suited you.'

Well you would, I thought, *seeing as you were Howard and in love with Henrietta.*

We got some drinks, hot chocolate for me and mint tea for Finn. He doesn't do caffeine or sugar apparently, all part of his fitness regime to keep looking good for the stage.

'So what did really you think of the article?' I asked as we settled back down.

'Like you were holding back. What you wrote was interesting, you've stated the facts, but I'd have liked a bit more of your personal reaction to it. What *you* were feeling and thinking.' He reached over and took my hand and I felt my insides lurch. 'Or are you scared to reveal the real you?'

'I . . .' He was looking directly into my eyes. I couldn't think straight. It didn't matter because he leant over and kissed me. Not a long kiss. More a brush of our lips, like a promise of things to come. I felt a rush from my toes to the top of my head. *If that's just an almost kiss, I can't wait to see what a proper kiss will feel like*, I thought.

We talked through some changes, though by then, I couldn't have cared less about the article. I was just happy being with Finn and knowing that we were on the brink of getting together. Finn looked at his watch. 'I have to go,' he said. 'Band practice. Have you time to walk with me to the bus stop?'

'Oh sure,' I said, and from the way he was looking at me and particularly at my mouth, I knew he meant so that we could be alone to continue our kiss.

We gathered our things, went outside and headed for the bus stop. Finn took my hand as we walked along and I felt light-headed from his touch. Once we reached the stop, he glanced down the road. I prayed that his bus didn't arrive on time. Luckily, there was no sign of it.

He moved closer to me, put his arm around me and pulled me to him. 'So, Jo Harris,' he said with a suggestive smile.

I blushed. 'So, Finn O'Brady.' I couldn't believe it was happening. Finn O'Brady right there with his arms around me. He moved in to kiss me and at last our lips met and a soft kiss became deeper and more intense.

What am I feeling? What am I feeling? I asked myself as Finn pushed his tongue into my mouth.

I feel like I'm kissing a slug! Urgh, this wasn't exactly the fireworks I was expecting and I wasn't sure I liked the way he smelt close up. It wasn't bad or unclean, more like caramel which was somehow too sweet. Our kiss continued and Finn crashed his mouth against mine, his lips open, full and wet . . . it didn't feel nice at all. Too sloppy and full on. And ergh, his tongue was sloshing around. I pulled back and had to resist the urge to wipe my chin with the back of my sleeve. Finn looked down at me with a pleased expression on his face. His bus arrived seconds later and as he got on board he turned back, pointed a finger and winked at me. 'Catch you later, Harris,' he said, then turned away to pay his fare.

Oh my God! Finn O'Brady is a knob, I thought as his bus pulled away. *How come I haven't seen it before? And a wet, sloppy kisser.* Effy and Tash had been so right. A kiss would be the test. Although Tash says that sometimes you have to teach a boy to kiss properly or they never learn. *But Finn must have kissed loads of girls*, I told myself. *Maybe none of them had ever had the nerve to tell him. Oh no. I don't know what I feel now. Do I want to catch him later? And coax him into kissing more gently?* I was surprised to find that I didn't think I did. I felt flat. *What shall I do?* I asked myself. *Talk to the girls*, my inner mind came back with. I got out my phone and texted both of them.

* * *

We met at Effy's half an hour later to discuss the situation.

'Oh dear,' said Effy. 'How are you going to tell him?'

'Don't,' said Tash. 'I think you should give him another chance and tell him how you like to be kissed.'

'But I don't know if I even know myself,' I said. I felt torn. To date Finn would be great kudos and I had to admit I liked the idea of being seen around with him. *But surely I should be feeling more if he's the great love of my life, my soulmate, or maybe we have to get used to each other. He might not have liked the way I kissed either. Maybe it's me who's not good at kissing. I felt Owen was too bland and Finn too full on so maybe it's not them, maybe it's me!* It was all so confusing. Why don't they teach this stuff in school?

Finn called the next day and suggested a date so maybe he was happy with my kissing technique after all. I agreed to see him again because I was seriously beginning to wonder if there was something wrong with *me*. For months, I'd had an almighty crush on Finn. Just a glance from him had been enough to make me tingle all over. But now that it was actually happening, I felt numb. Maybe I was incapable of love. A freak. I'd read magazine articles about commitment phobes, people who are scared of intimacy, who run away when things get real and always live in a fantasy world. I didn't want to be like that, plus there was still the chance that despite the first kiss let-down, Finn might be Howard. I felt that it was too soon to dismiss him from the list so I decided that I should give him another chance.

Curiously though, the thought of Ben was still nagging at the back of my mind too. I'd rewritten my part of the article as Finn had suggested and he seemed happy enough with what I'd done but I kept wondering what Ben would think of it. I emailed him asking if he'd like to take a look or discuss the photos for the article. He emailed back:

No need. Finn has approved and he's the boss. You'll see my photos soon enough in the maga-zine. Hope you're enjoying life with Finn.

Regards, Ben

Regards. How cold and business-like is that? I thought. I was surprised to find that I felt hurt by the fact that he didn't want to see me.

I spotted him the following Saturday with Max on the Heath. He had shades on so I wasn't sure if he saw me or not. Either way, he turned and headed off in the opposite direction. Not Max though. Max came bounding over to me and leapt up to lick my face like I was his oldest, dearest friend.

'Maybe you're Howard, Max. It would be just my luck that he'd be back as a dog,' I said.

'Woof,' Max agreed.

Ben whistled for him in the distance and Max ran off to join him. *He probably doesn't recognise me with my new haircut and clothes,* I told myself but deep inside I knew that he'd seen me. He just didn't want to talk to me.

Curiously, the more Ben didn't want to talk to me, the more I wanted to talk to him. When the article came out, his photos were great. He'd captured the characters perfectly. He'd done fabulous portraits that showed a sense of humour: Wind Dancer looking like she'd stab rather than heal someone, Annie surrounded by her pottery nick-nacks and her dog, and Lily having a fag and looking totally disinterested. I'd love to have asked his opinion of what he thought of them as people but as I studied the photos I thought, yeah, no need. His viewpoint was all there in the pictures.

During the last few weeks of term, Finn and I had been dating. All the usual places – back row at the cinema, picnics on the Heath, evening walks down by the river and mega snog sessions. Finn did like to kiss. I tried my best to encourage him to take it more slowly, but full on was his style and he always went back to the slug kiss. After a few weeks, I couldn't kid myself that things were going to improve and the chemistry I'd felt so intensely earlier in the term faded like ice in a microwave. Also, the more time I spent with him the more I realised that he liked his own way, and just as he was lead singer in the band, he liked to be the lead in our relationship. We went where he wanted to go, saw movies he wanted to see, and he talked about himself all the time. He never asked what I'd like to do and just assumed that I'd be happy with his choices. Once or twice, he asked a question about me, but always seemed to bring it back to himself again. It was the Finn O'Brady show on and off the stage. As for him being Howard, I looked deeply into his eyes time and again, searching for that spirit I'd seen looking out of the sepia photograph at Mrs Rayner's, but there was no recognition of anybody else in there but Finn, Finn and Finn.

When we finally broke up for the summer holidays and Finn told me of plans to go to Cornwall with his family, I took the opportunity to extract myself gently.

'I don't want you to feel tied down to me when you're away,' I said. 'Like, if you meet some hottie on the beach, and knowing you, you probably will, it will be better that you're free and don't feel like you'd be cheating.'

Finn laughed. 'It's true, there are a lot of hot girls down there.'

'And then you'll be off to uni in September,' I continued, 'and I definitely wouldn't want you to feel tied to me then and not to have fun in your first year.'

He got what I was saying. Finn wasn't stupid. 'Exactly what I was thinking. I wouldn't want you to feel tied either. No strings. Free agents. You're really cool, Jo Harris. Let's meet up when I get back from holiday and take it from there. Yeah?'

'Yeah.'

We both knew that we wouldn't.

Chapter Thirty

Owen came back from uni the weekend that Finn left for Cornwall. He suggested a walk on the Heath on the Sunday evening when Effy and Tash had gone to the movies with Dave and Mark.

'Effy's filled me on all the Henrietta stuff,' he said as we strolled down to the ponds. 'I'd love to see a photo of her.'

'Mrs Rayner let me do some copies,' I said and pulled the photo out of my bag to show him.

We sat on a bench overlooking the water and Owen studied the photo for a while. 'And you really believe that you were her?'

I nodded. 'I do. There's so much evidence that I can't ignore, especially the Katie Barrow part. What do you make of it all?'

He shrugged. 'Not sure. I've been thinking about it since Effy told me the latest. It could be that you're some kind of psychic yourself and tuned into Henrietta—'

'My mum said that.'

'It doesn't mean that you were her. There could be lots of explanations. I don't know. Personally, I wouldn't dwell on it too much if I were you. I mean, even if it was true, she's gone, in the past. *You're* here. That's what matters, this lifetime, the people that you meet this time and the choices that you make now.'

'Mum said that too! The here and now. That's what's important.'

'And I hear things are over with Finn?'

I nodded. 'Not The One after all.'

Owen laughed. 'I could have told you that.'

I laughed with him. 'I'm sure you could have.'

We got up, walked to the top of the hill and found another bench where we sat in a comfortable silence and watched the sun go down over London. He put his arm around me and it felt good to be with him. One of my oldest and best friends. As the sky in front of us turned to soft pinks, it felt like the perfect romantic moment and Owen turned to face me. He pulled me closer and kissed me on the lips. Owen is a good kisser, no doubt about it. Tender, not too full on, not too soft. It felt nice. Safe. But still zero chemistry. I felt so bad but it was time to be totally honest with him so that he could meet someone who would feel the same way about him.

'Owen?'

'Yes?'

'What you said just now about this life. I really hope you meet someone special who feels the same way about you,' I said.

'I thought I had,' he replied.

I took his hand and squeezed it. 'I do love you. I always will, Owen, but just . . .'

'Not in that way,' he finished for me and sighed.

I nodded. 'But . . . friends forever, please.'

He squeezed my hand back. 'Friends forever.'

'And sometimes friends can last longer than lovers,' I added.

He nodded and smiled, but I could see the sadness in his eyes. *Love is really tough*, I thought.

There is something seriously wrong with me, I decided once the sun had gone and we made our way back down the hill. *It's not Finn or Owen or anyone. It's* me. *I am incapable of feeling all that love forever stuff I've yearned for or maybe it's not even real. Maybe it only exists in books.*

At the bottom of the hill, Owen gave me a big hug and I hugged him back. A friendly hug. 'I *do* love you, Owen,' I said. 'I really meant that and we *will* be friends forever. I'll probably even feel a little jealous when you meet the true love of your life but until then, I just want you to know that I'll always be here for you.'

'Ditto,' he said and gently tried to push me away. 'Now move away. She may be watching and I don't want her to get the wrong idea.'

I hugged him even harder. 'She's going to have to get used to the idea. Love Owen, love his mates.'

'So that leaves Ben,' said Effy after I'd phoned her to fill her in.

'No it doesn't,' I said. 'It leaves a whole world of boys I've never even met yet. Ben doesn't even *like* me and I'm not sure I like him very much either any more. So I'm back to being a singleton. And actually . . . it feels good. I'd rather be on my own than in a relationship that isn't working like with Finn or with Owen and feeling guilty.'

'I guess,' said Effy. 'And I'm sure the real Howard will come along one day. In the meantime, there's nothing stopping you from dating other boys.'

'Exactly,' I said.

Chapter Thirty-one

The second week of the holidays, Effy and Tash had loads of plans – a visit to the Royal Academy in Piccadilly, a trip to Covent Garden, boating down at Richmond, but of course they'd be with Dave and Mark and I wasn't in the mood for being Miss Tag Along. On the Tuesday, Effy called to beg me to go to Greenwich with them but I told her I had jobs to do for Mum. I wasn't lying. Mum had a whole list of chores for me and I was glad to do them. Our relationship was so much better since the day I'd told her about Henrietta and we'd finally talked about Dad. Instead of feeling angry with her, I could see how hard she worked and wanted to help out.

It was a lovely warm day, too good to stay inside, so I walked up to Highgate to get some groceries from the shopping list that Mum had left me. First though, I decided to take a stroll in the park down the lane by the cemetery. As I made my way there, I couldn't help but feel that everything had turned out to be one great anticlimax. For weeks, it had felt like so much was unfolding in the Henrietta story but suddenly it had gone quiet and here I was, another holiday, my mates still both in their couple bubbles and me, once again, all by myself.

I sat on a bench and got out a bag of nuts that I'd brought to feed the squirrels when Max appeared at my feet and jumped up to give me a hello lick.

'Hi, Howard,' I said as I looked to my left to see if Ben was around.

'Howard? His name is Max,' said a voice behind me to my right.

I turned and there was Ben. He was dressed in his usual black T-shirt and jeans and wearing Ray-Ban aviators.

'Private joke between me and Max,' I said.

'So . . . how are you?' he asked.

'Good.'

'You look different.'

'Different good or different bad?'

'Good, definitely good. Not that you didn't look OK before but. . .'

'But what?'

'It was like you were living in another time, not this one.'

'Exactly,' I said. 'That's why I changed my look. Moving on.' I went back to feeding the squirrels, trying to look casual, hoping he might stay and chat.

My cool tactic didn't work because when I turned around to continue the conversation, I saw Ben disappearing round a corner in the distance. *Grrr*, I thought. *It wouldn't hurt him to have a polite conversation.*

When I'd finished feeding the squirrels, I got up to go. Despite my annoyance, I found myself looking to see if Ben was still in the park but there was no sign of either of him or Max. The more I thought about Ben, the more I realised that I'd missed a chance to get to know him better and I was surprised to find out how much I felt like I'd lost out. He made me laugh. He was creative. An animal lover. From the few conversations we'd had, I liked the way he thought. We could have had something. *He was interested in me at one point*, I told myself as I headed back up towards the village, *he definitely was. He wouldn't have sent me that card for my birthday and come to meet me in Highgate if he wasn't. And there was definitely a connection between us.* I could still remember how it felt when we'd looked into each other's eyes, but at the time I couldn't take the intensity of it and had looked away. I wondered what would have happened if I hadn't broken my gaze? Whatever. I'd clearly blown it with him. I'd been obsessing so much about Finn at the time, I wouldn't even have recognised Howard if he'd turned up on my front doorstep complete in Victorian dress and fallen at my feet.

Over the next weeks, I kept seeing Ben around north London, in the supermarket, in the street, and one day in Highgate tube station, he was going down the escalator as I was going up the stairs to his left. Coincidence or that synchronicity thing Effy was always on about. Whatever, it made no difference because he was always the same: unsmiling, unfriendly, shades on as if he was hiding behind them.

His loss, I told myself. *Boys. Who needs them?*

One night I was at home and I got out my photos of Henrietta and Howard. I gazed into Howard's eyes. 'Who are you? Where are you now?'

I put the photos back in my drawer then went to watch TV downstairs where I dozed off. I was back in the room where I'd first seen Henrietta. Howard was there. Too late. She didn't have long. 'I will find you,' he said. 'I will find you.' I gazed up into his eyes. I knew those eyes and suddenly, it wasn't Howard I was looking up at, it was Ben! Somehow his eyes were the same . . . I woke with a start. It was just a dream. A dream. *Ben Fraser, get out of my head*, I told myself. *I am not going to think of you any more, not even for a second.*

Despite my resolutions, I saw Ben the next morning. I was up in the village because I'd arranged to meet Effy at her mum's office and saw him across the road with Max. He did his usual number. About-turn, walk the opposite way. This time, I went after him.

'Why don't you like me?' I asked him when I'd caught up with him. Then I cringed. What was I thinking? Why don't you like me is number one question *not* to ask a boy you like. It comes across as desperate.

'Not like you? What makes you think that?'

'Duh. You're always scowling at me. You walk in the other direction whenever you see me, both clues I'd say.' *Shut up, shut up now*, my mind told me.

'Ever looked in the mirror? You scowl back.'

'Do not.'

'Do.'

I reached up to take his shades off.

Ben caught my wrist. 'What are you doing?'

'I need to see your eyes,' I said.

'My eyes? Why?' Ben look startled and took a step back. I realised that I probably appeared to be acting like a madwoman.

'Er . . . studying iridology. It's my new hobby. Please. Just a moment, let me look.'

Ben shrugged and took his Ray-Bans off.

He was taller than me so I stood on tiptoe so that I could look directly at him. I stared into his eyes and tried to see beyond his face, deep into his eyes to the spirit within. He didn't flinch but looked straight at me as well. As had happened back in the café weeks earlier, I felt a connection, like a magnet pulling us together. I know he felt it too. This time, I didn't break my gaze. I continued looking and the connection grew deeper to the point it felt like time had stood still and we were alone in the world. And suddenly there he was. Howard. A different face, different eyes but the spirit was the same. I couldn't help it. It was like seeing your dearest, best friend after not seeing them for ages. I felt ridiculously happy and grinned. It must have been infectious because Ben did too.

'What?' he asked. 'What's funny?'

'Nothing. Not funny. Just I feel happy because . . . I haven't seen you . . . er . . . for a while.' And then I couldn't help but laugh.

Ben shook his head in bewilderment. 'Harris, are you on drugs?'

'No. Don't think so. Um . . . so . . . Ben, do you, er . . . want to hang out sometime over the summer?'

Ben looked increasingly taken aback. 'Hang out sometime? Why now?'

'I . . . long story.'

'Because Finn's no longer available?'

'Oh that's over now.'

Ben nodded. 'Yeah, he told me that he'd finished it.'

'*He'd* finished it? What a cheek.'

'Didn't he?'

'It was mutual.'

'Right,' said Ben like he didn't believe me for a second. I guess not many girls broke up with Finn O'Brady, or maybe he never admitted it.

'So how about we meet up? I'd . . . I'd like to get to know you better,' I persisted.

By now, Ben appeared totally confused. He looked up and down the street then back at me. 'Just because you're over Finn now, doesn't mean you can just come and snap your fingers and I'll fall in line, Jo. Sorry. It doesn't work that way. Maybe there was a time when . . . never mind. Look, have a good summer, yeah?'

With that, he walked off with Max trotting after him. The joy of recognition I'd felt only moments earlier turned to panic at the thought that he might not feel the same as me after all. I'd taken that part for granted and never for a second imagined that we'd find each other and he'd say, so what? It couldn't be that I was going to get so close for him to walk away.

'*OI YOU!*' I called after him. He turned back. 'Yeah, you. Ben Fraser. I'm talking to you.' Inwardly I cringed again. What was I saying? I was breaking every code on how to be cool and behaving like a total stalker but I couldn't help myself. I breathed a sigh of relief when I saw that a glimmer of a smile crossed Ben's face. 'I don't expect to snap my fingers and you'll come running but . . . you *can't* reject me without a second thought.'

'I can,' he said but he laughed as he said it and took a few steps back towards me. 'You're very sure of yourself all of a sudden.'

'Not just myself. Of us. Sure of *us*.'

'*Us?* What us? There is no us.'

'Yes there is.'

'Since when?'

'Ah now that's a long story. Maybe I'll tell you one day. OK. Listen. I'm a bit slow sometimes and, when it comes to boys, I've got a lot to learn but I get this *really* strong feeling we're meant to be together.'

'Since when?' Ben repeated.

'Since lately.'

'And what if I don't share your impulse?'

'It's not an impulse, honestly. And I know you were interested. That time in the café you felt something and just now too. You must have felt it.'

Ben's expression darkened.

'I'm sorry,' I said. 'I know we didn't get off to a good start. I know that when I asked you about the boy I'd just met, you thought I was talking about you, didn't you?'

Ben looked away. 'But it was Finn, wasn't it? Always Finn.'

'My mistake. I know now, it's you, Ben, you. I . . . I've been looking for you for a *long* time, it just took me some time to recognise you.'

Ben whistled. 'Wow. Some chat-up line you got going for you there, Harris.'

I reached out and took his hand. 'Not a chat-up line. I mean it. Fate's given us a second chance. It really has. You have to believe it.'

'Jo, you're doing my head in,' he said softly then he shook his head, turned and began to walk away again.

As I watched him go, I felt wracked with pain and a cry came from somewhere deep inside. '*No, please. Come back to me, please.*' A couple of teenagers on the other side of the road glanced over, nudged each other, then walked on whispering. I knew how I looked – like a desperate saddo trying to hang on to a boy who didn't want to know. I didn't care. '*Ben!*' I called. I didn't care what anyone thought.

Ben walked a few more steps then he did turn and come back.

Before he could say anything, I moved towards him and kissed him gently. He didn't exactly respond but he didn't resist either. We pulled back and looked into each other's eyes. He seemed to be searching mine as if looking for an explanation but it wasn't the time for words. As we stood there, there was no denying the amazing feeling, like we were merging into each other, becoming one. I moved in again and kissed him more deeply and once again he responded. I wanted it to go on forever but after a while, we pulled back and looked at each other.

Ben looked so vulnerable, all trace of the cool guy gone. 'No games, Jo. I don't play games.'

I pulled him tighter to me and caught his scent. It was divine, a light citrus but something deeper too that made me melt. I wanted to lose myself in it. 'No games. Seriously, Ben. I didn't know it until recently but I've been looking for you for a long, long time, longer than I can explain at the moment.'

'And I've been waiting for you,' Ben whispered, as if afraid to say the words too loud.

'For me? Waiting?'

Ben nodded. 'I knew the first time I saw you that you were The One but then it was as if I became invisible to you.' He took a deep breath. 'I've felt a connection to you ever since that day I saw you hiding behind the changing rooms on the playing field. I felt right with you, like I belonged with you.'

'Why didn't you ever say something?'

'After that time, it was as if I didn't exist to you. I saw you a few times with your mates in Highgate. You didn't even register me and then later, there was always Finn somewhere around.'

'I'm sorry. I've been lost. In a dream. But I'm awake now and I've found you . . . You could call it love at second sight.'

This time it was Ben who leant forward to kiss me and a wave of pure happiness surged through me. He pulled back to look deep into my eyes again and inwardly, I felt something lift and the veils of time drew back. Howard and Henrietta were united, no longer trapped in the past. We were together in the present as Jo and Ben and from the way he was looking at me, the future was looking good for all of us.

Cathy Hopkins
Million Dollar Mates

"Perfect"
WONDROUS
READS

Moving in and moving up? Follow Jess as she joins the glitterati A-list...

"Girly Fun!"
BLISS
MAGAZINE

Cathy Hopkins
Million Dollar Mates
Cathy Hopkins
Million Dollar Mates
Paparazzi Princess
COMING SOON . . . SUPERSTAR
Cathy Hopkins
Million Dollar Mates
Catwalk Queen
Cathy Hopkins
Million Dollar Mates
Golden Girl

Cathy Hopkins

Exclusive news and gossip

Sign up for the Cathy Hopkins newsletter

Enter glam competitions

Connect with other Cathy fans

Read Cathy's Blog

There are lots of ways to keep up-to-date with the latest news and info on Cathy and her books online . . .

Visit www.cathyhopkins.com
and www.milliondollarmatesbooks.co.uk

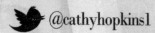 Search for The Official Cathy Hopkins group on Facebook

@cathyhopkins1

facebook

Sign Up | The OFFICIAL Cathy Hopkins Group i
Sign up for Facebook to connect with Th

The OFFICIAL C

Cathy Hopkins
Bestselling author of Mates.

Wall | Info | D

Cathy Hopkins
Million Dollar Mates

"Cathy Hopkins writes like a dream."
myfavouritebooks.blogspot.com

Events | About | Competition

et short, timely mee
Twitter is a rich source of instantly
incredibly wide variety of topics. Joi

Sign Up ›

Get updates on new, fabulously glam micro-site (how very posh,
-site!) The purpose of this link is to give you all
es, *Million Dollar Mates*. Be the first to read
up, check out covers, gen up on characters,
much more as it develops. I hope you like it!
ye for now, Cathy X

 CathyHopkins1

twitpic   out -
st
Cathy Ho

y Hopkins   Sign
newsle

Books | About Cathy | Blog | Gallery | Downloads

welcome to my website.

of stuff on here so do have a look round by pressing on the
you know how it goes! You never know what you might find:
photo of my cats, covers from different countries around the
ing those), my tip top writing tips, all the latest goss about
il sorts. Have a wander. Hope you enjoy! Cathy X

It's set in a glamorous
partment complex – No 1,
ter Park in
ndon. Jess

Cathy H
Twi

About the Author

Cathy Hopkins lives in Bath, England with her husband and three cats, Dixie, Georgia and Otis. Cathy has been writing since 1986 and started writing teenage fiction in 2000. She spends most of her time in her writing turret pretending to write books but is actually in there listening to music, hippie dancing and checking her facebook page. So far Cathy has had fifty three books published, some of which are available in thirty three languages.

She is looking for the answers to why we're here, where we've come from and what it's all about. She is also looking for the perfect hairdresser. Apart from that, Cathy has joined the gym and spends more time than is good for her making up excuses as to why she hasn't got time to go. You can visit her on Facebook, or at www.cathyhopkins.com